TITLE
ALPHA'S LOVER

One

SASHA

"Run child."

"Be that as it may, momma I'm worn out!"

"I know darling, yet we need to go. I really want you to run."

Sasha was going through the timberland attempting frantically to keep her hand held in her mom's. Her little four-year-old legs were struggling keeping up.

"Elsie, thusly."

Sasha went to see her dad to one side, enticing them to come to him. Her mom scooped Sasha up in her arms and held her nearby as she ran toward her better half.

"Is it safe to say that they are following us?"

"They said they'd give us until the morning to get off the pack lands. We should arrive at the south boundary in an hour assuming we shift. I'll convey Sasha."

Sasha was lifted onto her dad's back whenever he had moved into his wolf and she clutched onto his hide as her folks dashed against the sun toward the south boundary. She floated off to rest, ignorant about exactly how much her life planned to change.

"MISS LOVETT I NEED THOSE PAPERS IN HERE NOW!"

"Indeed, coming!" I hollered as I ran from my work area. This man was angering, best case scenario, and it took each ounce of my wolf not to tear the man's throat out day by day. Mr Bettany was a short, bold human with a noisy mentality and little regard for his workers.

"About time..." he frowned as he grabbed the papers from my hands.

I needed to stop, to truly take advantage of this jerk that I was finished with the obnoxious attack and that he wanted me an overabundance him. Yet, that was completely false. I really wanted this work. I had no other person to deal with me.

"Please accept my apologies for the stand by, Mr. Bettany. Is there something else you really want?"

"No," he protested, shooing me away with his hand. I took a seat at my work area and let out a full breath.

Is it true or not that you are certain we can't kill him?

I giggled discreetly at my wolf Raya's remark. "If by some stroke of good luck!" I murmured.

Assuming I was being straightforward I realized I shouldn't say anything negative. This wasn't even the most noticeably awful work I'd at any point had. Functioning as a janitor at a spa was certainly at the first spot on the list. Individuals are really sickening.

However, i was consistently watching out for another work. One that would offer greater strength and security, perhaps an increase in salary. It would be great to have the option to bear the cost of a superior condo. Or on the other hand even essential things like some new garments and yummy food.

"Miss Lovett!"

Feigning exacerbation, I remained from my work area and advanced into Mr. Bettany's office, ensuring I put on that phony assistance grin I had consummated. "Indeed, Mr. Bettany?"

"I have a gathering at 9am tomorrow first thing. You will set up the meeting room and ensure everything is awesome. Here are the subtleties."

I took the record from Mr. Bettany and with a "yes sir" advanced back to my work area. I realized a 9am gathering implied I would need to come in ahead of schedule to set up the room-something I wasn't anticipating. Mr Bettany wasn't by and large known for compensating double time energetically. I chose to make things as simple for myself as could be expected, making the essential duplicates in general and booklets for the gathering currently so all I'd need to do tomorrow is acquire the espresso truck and spot the documents on the table.

I gazed toward the clock a couple of hours after the fact to see that it was right around five.

"Thank goodness..." I muttered, snatching my jacket and tote prior to thumping on the entryway of my manager's office. "Something else you want today, Mr. Bettany?"

"No. You can go."

"Goodnight, sir," I presented happily prior to leaving the workplace and advancing toward the lift.

When the entryways shut I breathed out and inclined toward the rail. "I really want to go for a run."

Goodness gosh, please!! It's been ages! Raya cried.

I chuckled, "We just went on Tuesday."

A day and a half is longer than it ought to be.

I feigned exacerbation. "Fine. In any case, no moving in mud this time-do you have any idea that it was so abnormal to stroll once more into the high rise like that?" I could feel Raya laugh at the memory.

Being a maverick implied I didn't have the advantage of running on secured lands. I needed to agree to a half hour drive to the closest state park and trust no one saw me. It likewise implied I was unable to go as frequently as I would like. Fortunately going to the rec center took a portion of the edge off. I came to my condo and changed into something agreeable prior to looking at my telephone on my way.

No new messages. "Feel sorry for.." I murmured, trusting somebody had responded to one of my many applications.

"Surmise I truly need to return to work tomorrow."

Subsequent to driving the half hour to the state park and peeling off my garments I moved, feeling the opportunity and arrival of the shift.

"Keep in mind... no mud!"

Raya gave a lively snarl before we hustled off into the forest. We ran for a really long time, pursuing irregular natural life and sprinkling in a stream prior to advancing back to the vehicle. I moved back, my breath battered from the run as I got dressed and drove home.

Subsequent to showering the remaining parts of my run off my body I hurled myself on the bed, a casual murmur getting away from my lips. Running was a high yet quieting at the same time. I wanted to go all the more regularly.

Possibly when we observe our mate we will get to go at whatever point we need, Raya said ideally, hearing my musings.

"I don't believe that is truly going to occur," I answered as I floated off to rest.

TWO

SASHA

"Whyyyy?" I moaned as I smacked my caution. I scoured my face, completely lamenting going on that run final evening. I realized I must be up sooner than expected yet remained out beyond two AM.

"I fault you," I heaved at Raya as I rearranged up to shower and get dressed. I knew there was a gathering today and expected to attempt to put my best self forward. I just had seven days of outfits yet there was one that was undeniably more pleasant than the rest and I saved it for occasions such as this when Mr. Bettany needed us to all do our absolute best.

With a pack of bagels and arranged cakes in a single hand and the espresso I had been savoring an endeavor to liven myself up in the other, I entered the workplace. I set up the meeting room and came to my work area similarly as Mr. Bettany showed up.

"Good day, Mr. Bettany," I ringed in an agreeable tone.

"Gee.." he muttered prior to strolling into his office.

I plunked down and started working when the telephone at my work area rang.

"Gold Form Logistics, Mr. Bettany's office."

"Hello Sasha, it's Paul. Simply needed to tell you your 9am is on its way up."

"Much appreciated hun." Paul was the best sixty year elderly person you could possibly do meet. He worked the security work area in the hall and I had favored him the moment I met him.

"Mr Bettany, your 9am gathering is on their way up."

"Indeed, yes. Much thanks to you Miss Lovett."

I pulled out of the room in shock, he never said thanks to me. Ever.

I assembled my things and hung tight for Mr. Bettany to advance out to the meeting room. As we strolled up I could see through the glass that they were holding nothing back there pausing.

Mr Bettany opened the entryway, "Courteous fellow, thank you for coming out."

I strolled through entryway however halted right away. I was stuck to the spot. My head gobbled up to take a gander at the men in the room. I could smell them, I knew what they were. Out of nowhere, every man in that room moved their look to me and I realized they could smell me. They knew what I was. I could feel the bunch in my stomach.

They are all from a similar pack. You can guess by their smell, Raya said delicately, the hairs on the rear of my neck standing up as she woke up.

I gestured my head inside, incapable to do anything.

"Miss Lovett, the entryway," Mr. Bettany protested, waking up me from my shock. I dropped my head and plunked down in my seat close to the back divider to take notes.

At the point when the gathering was over I hurried out of the room and back to my work area.

"Try not to freeze, perhaps they're simply going through with an arrangement and you will not at any point need to see them once more," I muttered, holding my head down and attempting to console myself. I had gone over my reasonable part of packs and I realized how forceful they could be. I had the scar on my ribcage to demonstrate it. They would rather avoid rebels, regardless of how youthful or vulnerable they were.

"Miss Lovett, right?"

I smelled him before I even turned upward. I raised my eyes to meet his. "Uh… yes. Would i be able to help you?"

I gazed toward the man before me. He was tall and genuinely attractive. He had short, brownish hair and a splendid face and I could feel his essence. Whatever he was, he was a high position in their pack.

"I am Jim Thorpe, I work for TITAN Corporation. Assuming there is anything that you really want, call me." He gave me his card and I gazed at him in disarray.

"For what reason would I do that?" I asked, attempting to comprehend the reason why this arbitrary wolf was offering benevolence, particularly to me.

"We are buying Gold Form Logistics. You will presumably be out of a task."

"Be that as it may, for what reason would you need me?" I glanced around to be certain no people were tuning in, "I'm not a piece of your pack."

He grinned and gestured his head, "Valid." He dismissed to walk, halting at the lift, "I'll anticipate your approach Monday."

There were no words. In a real sense, I was unable to track down anything to say I just stayed there in shock.

Is it safe to say that we are getting a pack?! Raya shouted.

"Quiet yourself. We aren't getting a pack. He just extended to us an employment opportunity, I don't think I'll even take it." I could feel Raya feign exacerbation at me, aggravated with my wavering.

That evening and the entire end of the week I was anxious. I didn't have the foggiest idea what to do. It made me wish my father was here. He had forever been so great at quieting me when I overthought things. In any case, early Monday morning I discovered some lucidity. I got my telephone and dialed the number on the card.

"What the heck am I doing?" I asked myself as I heard the telephone ring.

"Jim Thorpe."

"Greetings, Mr. Thorpe this is Sasha Lovett from Gold Form."

"Ok! Miss Lovett! I was hanging tight for your call. I trust it's to let me know you need a task!"

I let out a full breath and shut my eyes.

Could it be said that you are certain with regards to this?

"Not in the slightest degree," I inside answered to my wolf, "Yet we're going to be jobless with no different possibilities."

"Indeed. I'd cherish a task."

THREE

SASHA

After seven days I strolled in for my first day at TITAN Corporation. I could feel the strength of the pack the moment I strolled into the structure. It was practically devastating. Each maverick cell in my body was willing me, beseeching me, to run. Taking this occupation conflicted with all that I had been shown growing up and my dad's words reverberated to me.

"A pack is hazardous, never trust a pack."

"Assuming that you get found out in their domain you'll be killed."

"Try not to attempt to prevail upon them, recently run"

"We are generally the pack we will at any point require."

I woke up myself from my recollections and advanced toward the hall gathering. The young lady at the work area gave me a sniff and a glower. "Would i be able to help you?"

"Hey, I'm here to see Jim Thorpe."

"Furthermore you are?" She found me and down, attempting to sort out on the off chance that I was truly expected to be there.

"Sasha Lovett."

She peered toward me prior to getting the telephone, "Miss Lovett to see Beta Thorpe. Mhmmm.." She hung up the telephone and checked out me once more, "Alright, Miss Lovett. Take the lift to the eighth floor, Mr. Thorpe will be sitting tight for you."

"Much thanks to you," I answered, allowing my words to trickle with benevolence.

"Miss Lovett! So happy to see you!" Mr. Thorpe tolled as I left the lift. I shook his hand cheerfully, "Great morning Mr. Thorpe."

"Good gracious, call me Jim, everybody does."

I answered with a gesture, not certain assuming I was prepared at this point to definitely call him that.

"OK, so Mr. Bettany said that you, and I quote, 'weren't the most noticeably terrible associate he's had' which from what I assemble of Mr. Bettany is essentially a gleaming survey."

That made me laugh and I let out a breath, "You can't really understand."

"All things considered, assuming you had the option to endure Mr. Bettany than this ought to be easy. You'll be the new colleague for our CEO and Alpha, Jackson Thorpe."

"Thorpe as in..." My eyes squinted as my cerebrum attempted to make the association.

"My sibling."

"Ahh," I answered with a gesture of the head. This shouldn't be really awful, assuming he's in any way similar to Jim he'll be a way preferable manager over the old savage, Mr. Bettany.

"I'll provide you with the fabulous visit through the spot. Here is the lunchroom. The refrigerator is constantly loaded, kindly grab whatever. There's espresso and tea and other arbitrary beverages and tidbits. Here is the document room and duplicate room. We have two primary board rooms on this floor. This one here by my office and the second a few doors down nearer to yours. How about we take you to your work area and we can go over your agreement."

"Much obliged to you," I grinned and followed him down the corridor to a huge arrangement of swinging doors with a spotless, present day work area positioned right external them.

"Here we are. Pull up a chair and investigate the agreement, I will go illuminate him you're here." He left and I peered down at the record in my grasp and opened it, perusing the terms. My eyes broadened at the rundown of rules and specifications, generally going over the way that I would manage private business and pack matters and couldn't offer them to anybody. In any case, my eyes became significantly more extensive at the lower part of the page where it expressed my compensation. That number couldn't really be correct. I would get more cash-flow than I'd at any point had.

Tragically, the dividers weren't exceptionally thick and I heard everything in the workplace, pulling me away from the wonderment of my agreement.

"Is it true or not that you are significant, Jimmy?!"

"Simply listen to me, Jack!"

"You can't employ a damn rebel to work for the pack! Would you be able to envision how she'll manage the entirety of our data?"

"She appears to be a sweet young lady and dependable. Wouldn't you say it's somewhat dismal that she's a rebel thus youthful? We could help her."

I brought down my head, I realized this wasn't going to work, that this had been unrealistic.

"She goes, Jimmy!"

"Jackson, she's remaining."

"We'll see concerning that!" He snarled and I could hear weighty strides coming toward me. The entryway flew open and unexpectedly the world started to turn. The aroma hit me with a crushing weight as wise and bergamot filled my faculties. It was inebriating. I admired meet the eyes of who I accept that was Jackson Thorpe.

"MATE!"

Mate! Mate! Mate! Mate!! I could hear Raya going off the deep end in my mind, yet my body wouldn't move.

It isn't so much that I didn't need a mate, I simply didn't think I really had one. At the point when I was more youthful everything I could contemplate was tracking down a mate to take me to his pack and make a home with me. Somebody to give me a protected spot. Yet, that second won't ever come. Presently I was 24 and it was for all intents and purposes incomprehensible for a wolf to go above and beyond tracking down a mate So I had surrendered. I could deal with myself, I was all the pack I want.

My psyche was snapped back to the world when I heard a low snarl. I admired see Jackson Thorpe standing forcefully above me. "You. Are. Not. My. Mate."

I brought down my head, trusting my accommodation would quiet him.

"No chance!"

I dashed my eyes up to see Jim feeling overwhelmed. "See! I told you employing her was smart!" He snickered and I was unable to help the little grin that tracked down its direction all over It was immediately eradicated by Jackson's snarl.

"We are not mates," Jackson heaved.

"What's more I disdain young doggies."

Jackson and I went to Jim, disarray apparent on our appearances.

"Gracious, I thought we were going near and making statements that weren't accurate," Jim shrugged with a smile, "My awful."

I attempted to smother a chuckle which just took his red hot look back to me. "In my office, both of you."

He raged back in to his office, Jim and I following behind. We sat in the seats opposite his work area and he reclined in his seat. I could see the battle inside him, I simply didn't have a clue what to do.

"Alpha Jackson, I would rather not "

Jackson intruded on me with a lift of his hand, "Don't talk."

We sat peacefully for seemingly everlastingly before he talked once more, "This is the thing that we will do. You will be my partner. I allow you one month. I don't expect you'll endure that long, I allow it seven days tops."

"Stand by, so I'm not terminated?" I asked in shock.

"Not yet."

"Also you will keep her as your mate?!" Jimmy added.

"Not yet."

My heart sunk. Each fantasy I'd had about observing a mate had simply kicked the bucket. I had never pondered what might occur on the off chance that he didn't need me.

"We'll see," he added.

That is not as awful... Raya whimpered.

"No one discusses this. I mean it Jimmy, in the event that you tell anyone I'll give a thumping to you."

"You'll attempt," he sneered.

Jackson stood, utilizing the full impact of his Alpha presence. "No one will talk about this. Do we have an understanding both of you?"

We both brought down our heads, "Yes."

"Great, presently return to work."

FOUR

JACKSON

"MATE!" my wolf Blaize pretty much shouted.

"That is incomprehensible!" I shouted in my mind.

Our mate is so wonderful! What's more she smells so gooooood! Blaize had gone from an in-your-face Alpha to an infatuated doggy in a brief instant.

"She's a damn rogue..." I mumbled as I sat in my office. When the young lady and Jim had left I expected to require a moment. I had abandoned tracking down a mate I was right around 26. Presently I know why. Clearly my mate was some insane rebel chick that figured out how to get everything she might want into my organization.

"I don't confide in her," I snarled.

Would we be able to see her once more?

"No!" I shouted. I had given them my terms. I wasn't going to dismiss her yet. I would give it a couple of days, or possibly I would give her a couple of days. She wasn't going to keep going long.

I murmured and remained from my seat, snatching my work area telephone as I advanced around the work area.

"Miss Lovett, my office."

"Indeed, sir."

After a second she strolled in and I was indeed hit with honeysuckle and vanilla. Her smell made me dazed. I needed to breathe in every last bit of her.

"How would i be able to help you, Mr. Thorpe?"

"Take these documents and sort them into their right spot in the record room. Then, at that point, take these and make duplicates of them, I want twelve of each document for a gathering tomorrow."

"Indeed, sir," she answered.

"Indeed, Alpha."

She gazed toward me like I was an insane individual, "Please accept my apologies?"

"It's Alpha to you."

I could see the fire rage through her eyes. "Indeed, Alpha," she gritted happily prior to turning and leaving my office.

"Noteworthy," I murmured to myself. At the point when I recognized that rage easily I thought without a doubt we'd have a show, yet she got control it over.

A couple of hours after the fact I understood I hadn't conveyed the update for the pack meeting. "Poo," I mumbled.

Miss Lovett,

Send an email about tomorrow night's pack meeting.

7pm at the pack house. Supper to follow.

Jackson Thorpe

I progressed forward with my work when I heard a ding on my work area.

Email sent.

I gazed toward the clock to see it was right around five. I snatched my things and advanced out of the workplace.

"Goodnight, Miss Lovett," I muttered.

"Goodnight, Mr. Thorpe," she answered, her voice was cool which I observed I didn't appreciate. In any case, I wasn't going to tell her that.

I pretty much hurried to the vehicle. I expected to move out of here and away from that young lady. I pulled out of the carport and made the brief commute home. Our pack house was on around twenty sections of land that we formally possessed, however we reared up to an enormous timberland. It was helpful and ok for our pack. It had been a long time since anything enormous had occurred and we were protected and agreeable. As I arrived at home I could feel myself unwind. I realized what might quiet me. The second I ventured from the vehicle I moved, not thinking often about the broke suit I left behind.

I'm not sure why you're battling this, Blaize muttered as we ran.

"I'm attempting to NOT ponder today. Wouldn't we be able to simply have a run?" I addressed furiously. Blaize reacted with a fit prior to driving into his run and dashing off through the back backwoods. At the point when I returned to the pack house I pulled on an extra pair of shorts and strolled through the secondary passage. It was late in the evening and supper had since quite a while ago passed. I rearranged through the kitchen, attempting to track down something that would really merit eating prior to heading higher up Nothing.

"Grain it is then, at that point," I mumbled to myself as I snatched a bowl and a spoon. Subsequent to eating a large portion of a container of Cocoa Puffs I advanced toward my space to shower and change.

"Alpha." The steamy voice occupied my room the second I entered.

"I don't have the tolerance for this evening. Leave," I protested, strolling past the bare she-wolf in my bed and entering the washroom. I don't have the foggiest idea why each and every female in this pack assumed it was OK to simply give themselves access to my room however it had never worked and it wasn't going to work this evening. There was dependably some wolf attempting to entice me in trusts I'd like her and make her the Luna. However, that is not how I work. I showered off the residue of my run uniquely to think that she is as yet in my bed.

"Leave. I will not ask once more," I said icily prior to strolling into the wardrobe to change. I required a couple of additional minutes trusting she would be gone when I got out. Fortunately she was and I had the option to fall into my bed and catch some rest before the morning came too soon.

"Hello, Alpha!" They all sang as I entered the pack kitchen.

"Good day," I grinned. I wish I could simply go the entire day, consistently here. However, I need to part my time between the pack lands and the pack business in the city.

Discussing pack business... when are we going to see our mate once more?!

I inside feigned exacerbation. My wolf was behaving like a little puppy all infatuated over that rebel. I ran my hands through my hair, "I don't have the foggiest idea how I will manage her." Even at the notice of that lady my psyche went wild thinking about her. Despite the fact that she was a rebel there was no question she was lovely. I shook the thought out about my head, I didn't have to get up to speed contemplating her.

Fortunately today was one of the days I spent at the pack and I wouldn't need to see her again until tomorrow.

FIVE

SASHA

I sat at my work area the entire daytime hanging tight for Mr. Thorpe to show up. When eleven o'clock came around I meandered a few doors down to Jim's office and tapped on the entryway.

"Mr Thorpe?"

He turned upward cheerfully and a wave,

"Please, it's Jim. It's just Mr. Thorpe when we have customers around. Come in. How would i be able to help you?"

"Indeed, I surmise my inquiry is truly how would i be able to help you?" I answered. He took a gander at me inquisitively so I proceeded. "Mr Thorpe hasn't as yet come in toward the beginning of today and I see his timetable is cleared so I sort of sit around aimlessly."

Jim let out a chuckle and ran a hand through his hair. "My gosh, he didn't tell you?"

"Let me know what?"

"He just comes to the workplace on Monday, Wednesday, and Friday."

I'm certain the expression all over was funny. "Then, at that point, what does he want me for?"

"Well clearly for the three days he's here, however when he's not in the workplace he wants you handling calls and demands from customers. Anything requiring a close down you ship off me for endorsement."

I let out a murmur, "Okay, I thought I had missed something."

Jim grinned energetically at me, "He can be somewhat of a grouch some of the time however he's the best Alpha our pack has had in many years."

"Truly?" I answered, truly doubting he was everything except acrid.

Jim gestured accordingly. "I can't imagine that our dad was certifiably not a dastardly elderly person that scarcely focused on the pack. He nearly drove us into the ground. However, Jackson chose us up from nothing and developed us to where we are today in only six years. Presently we're one of the most amazing ensured packs nearby and one of the top security firms in the Southeast, perhaps even on the east coast and our pack is all around accommodated."

I let out a dazed moan, "That is noteworthy."

"It is. So in any case, on Tuesdays, Thursday's, and toward the end of the week he is once again at the pack doing his Alpha thing. Yet, there will forever be one of us here during the week, worry don't as well."

"Much obliged to you," I gave him a comforting grin and advanced back to my work area and plunked down with perfect timing to receive a message.

Miss Lovett,

We have a few gatherings tomorrow. There are booklets
around my work area for each-if it's not too much trouble,
make duplicates and have the gathering room set up at nine
for the principal meeting.

Jackson Thorpe.

Subsequent to perusing his email I figured I should answer,
particularly since I couldn't say whether he was the sort of
host to offer rewards.

Mr Thorpe,

I will make the important duplicates and have everything
set up. Would you like me to set up rewards also?

S. Lovett

I stood and strolled into his office to recover the records he
had referenced and in the wake of observing them I took
them to the duplicate room where I began the printer prior
to checking my messages once more.

No to rewards for the first aside from possibly a pitcher or two of water. It will be a fast gathering. The subsequent one will be a lunch meeting. Make a request for twelve individuals. We will eat at precisely 12:30.

Thorpe

"Alright then, at that point," I said prior to driving away from the work area and strolling back to the duplicate room. Subsequent to making the booklets and taking my lunch I got back to track down a note around my work area

I came up to see you when I heard you had gotten employed here also. They gave me a spot down in the security room watching cameras. See you around desserts.

-Paul

That made my entire soul grin. Essentially I had one companion here. I gave careful consideration to discover where he was and visit him tomorrow on my lunch. My considerations were hindered by the telephone and subsequent to handling a couple of requires the remainder of the day it was at last an ideal opportunity to return home. I sat back in my seat and let out a breath, "Thank heavens."

I have found that there is one thing a wolf isn't intended to do and that is sit in a seat from morning 'til night.

I snatched my duffel bag and changed prior to going to the rec center to polish off my evening. I had never been prepared as a warrior yet I realized I expected to secure myself later a few narrow escapes before. I had taken self preservation classes and my new most loved thing at the rec center was kick boxing. Also most days it was actually what I expected to deliver the entirety of my repressed energy.

Later the class I headed back home sweat-soaked and loose, Raya was done pacing to be let out. I entered my little condo and snatched a container of extra Chinese takeout from the ice chest, taking it with me to the room as I changed.

As I stayed there eating my telephone rang and I peered down to see it was, in all honesty, Jackson Thorpe. I swallowed, there couldn't really be a valid justification he was calling at right around nine PM.

"Hi?" I addressed meekly.

"Miss Lovett," the voice on the opposite end snarled.

"Mr Thorpe, how would i be able to help you?"

"You can let me know how in the world we have a security break at the workplace!" he shouted into the telephone.

"Please accept my apologies?"

"There has been a security break. Somebody has taken grouped pack data off our server. Any estimates regarding who has done that?"

I knew where this was going at this point. It was inevitable. Turns out I had just a brief time prior to being faulted for something.

"Sir, there is by all accounts a slip-up here. I haven't taken anything," I answered, attempting to keep my voice level and quiet.

"Gracious, there's no mix-up. Do you truly anticipate that I should accept that we've never had a server break and afterward abruptly there is one only days later you show up?" he spat, and I could perceive he was furious.

"Mr Thorpe, I-"

"I will be at the workplace quickly, you should be holding up outside." He hung up the telephone and I let out a murmur. This will be a drawn out night.

"I should likely beginning searching for a task now..." I murmured.

Subsequent to changing out of my nightgown and into some thin pants and a free top I headed to the workplace. I really focused the entire way there, attempting to sort out assuming I had even dealt with anything arranged in my entire two days there. I hadn't. The main things I had done were on the business end of my occupation generally duplicate work and recording and accepting calls.

I remained external the structure trusting that my supervisor will show up, apprehensively picking at my nails as I remained there trusting I'd escape the present circumstance alive. I knew why I was being accused. It wasn't on the grounds that I was new.

A vehicle abruptly halted fiercely before the structure and an exceptionally irate Alpha strolled past me and to the entryways of the structure.

"Higher up, Miss Lovett."

I brought down my head and followed him to the lifts, understanding that I was being flanked by two other pack individuals.

"This is it. To this end Dad advised me to avoid packs. I'm dead."

SIX

JACKSON

"Alpha!" I heard over the brain connect, my head of safety for all intents and purposes hollering in my ears.

"What is it?" I protested.

"We have a security break!"

"At the boundary?! Was it taken care of? Is it safe to say that anyone was harmed?"

"No, sir! At TITAN. We just got a ready, somebody more likely than not gotten onto the pack server and taken a lot of private pack data."

"THEY WHAT?!"

In the thirty years this organization had been around there had not even once been a security break.

"Let them know I'm coming. Lock down the structure. No one goes in or out without my say!"

"Indeed, Alpha."

I got my telephone, I knew precisely who did this. It was absolutely impossible that that the week I let Jimmy convince me to recruit a maverick that unexpectedly there's a server break. I was astonished when she seemed as she didn't have the foggiest idea what I was discussing. I suppose you don't get by as a maverick without some very great acting abilities.

I saw Sasha remaining external the structure and the moment I ventured from the vehicle I smelled her. Honeysuckle and vanilla. It drove me much more mad. "Higher up, Miss Lovett."

She followed me up and I left the two men I had carried with me outside the entryway. I scarcely made it past the limit of my office before I lost it.

"WHERE ARE THE FILES?" I blast.

"I don't have them," she answered. Her voice was quiet and even, which just made me angrier.

"What do you mean you don't have them? Who did you offer them to?"

"No one. Since I didn't take them!" she raged.

There it was. The indignation. I could utilize her dissatisfaction for my potential benefit. I could make her bothered and befuddled.

"So you didn't sell them?"

"No."

"Then, at that point, where could they be?"

"Which part of 'I didn't take them' are you not getting?" She shouted and I stood straight, no little rebel planned to address me like that. Ordering all of my Alpha presence, I realized she would need to reply assuming that I inquired.

"Sasha, where-"

"Sir!" My gamma raged in holding a PC. "We tracked down
them

I shook off my evident disarray and sat at my work area.
"You tracked down the documents

"No, we observed who took them."

"I definitely realize who took them," I answered, projecting a
dull glare toward Sasha.

"The cameras got them. One of the recently added team
members from Gold Form."

I glared up at Sasha. Presently we had verification of her
double dealing. "Care to watch, Miss Lovett?" I grinned.

"Try not to care either way if I do," she heaved prior to
strolling over gladly, behaving like she wasn't gotten. We as
a whole accumulated around the screen as the clasp played.

My eyes augmented as the clasp showed a youngster in the
server room taking the documents. From the side of my eye
I could see Sasha fix gradually.

"Much thanks to you Ryan, if it's not too much trouble, find
that young fellow and bring him here promptly," I muttered
and my Gamma gestured his head and let us be.

I looked over to her to think that she is breathing weighty
and her face firm. I turned upward and I could see the
resentment beating through her and I could see the wolf
taking steps to be delivered.

"Crap..." I contemplated internally.

"Miss Lovett, I-"

I was halted when she pummeled her hands around my
work area. It was somewhat forceful. It angered the Alpha
in me.

"Sasha, you should watch-"

"Did you blame me since I'm new or on the grounds that I'm a maverick?" she murmured.

I faltered, not knowing how to react. She breathed in forcefully. "You packs are no different either way. You behave like we are largely beasts. You carry on like we are these horrendous, childish, crazy things that just cause damage."

I stood up, I wasn't going to allow this young lady to patronize me. I was her chief. "Miss Lovett, I lament erroneously blaming you for these activities yet "

"You lament erroneously charging me?!" She let out a jeer and I could experience the resentment spilling out of her. "You accused me since I'm a maverick!! You scared me, embarrassed me, put down me, and afterward dismissed it with a 'my terrible!'"

I could feel myself letting completely go and I could see her taking on a similar conflict. We were seconds from destroying this office. That couldn't occur here.

I took a full breath, "Miss Lovett, I am unfortunately allowed me to remind you we actually need to remain to some degree proficient in this structure. I'm still your chief and still your Alpha."

"You. Are. NOT. My. Alpha," she snarled.

That was the last bit of excess that will be tolerated. I stood up, my full presence transmitting, "Excuse me?"

She brought down her head yet not in genuine accommodation. It was all the more barely bitterly, "As you expressed previously, I'm a rebel. YOU are not my Alpha. I have no Alpha."

"Be that as it may, I am your chief!" I raged. "What's more to have some work tomorrow you ought to recollect that!"

She didn't reply yet I could see my words had produced their ideal results. There was a thump on the entryway and I could feel Jimmy attempting to mind connect me, "Jack, we have him outside."

"Acquire him," I answered in my mind prior to checking out Sasha who I could see was as yet irate as could be. "Goodnight, Miss Lovett."

She accepting a full breath like she needed to go another couple of rounds however at that point turned rapidly and surged out the entryway.

I could hear Jim outside the entryways as she left, "Hello, Sasha! Goodness, is everything...."

The men strolled in with the man that had caused this entire wreck and Jim sprung up to me once more. "What the heck is off-base with Sasha?"

"Nothing."

I could see his eyes extend as his psyche started interfacing specks. "Jack, you didn't."

"She's a rebel Jimmy! What other end would it be a good idea for me to have come to?"

I heard him let out a low snarl and gazed toward him. "You're a simpleton Jack," he tossed out over the psyche connect prior to putting the man down in a seat before my work area. I shook him off of my mind and zeroed in on the main pressing issue. I reclined in my seat and collapsed my arms, scowling at him hard.

"So Mr. Jones, need to let me know what was so intriguing in the server room today?"

SEVEN

SASHA

„Run child."

„However, momma I'm drained!"

„I know darling, yet we need to go. I really want you to run."

I was going through the timberland attempting frantically to keep my hand held in my mom's. My little four-year-old legs were battling to keep up and I could feel myself slipping.

„Elsie, along these lines.“

I went to see my dad to one side, coaxing us to come to him. My mom scooped me up in her arms and held me close as she ran toward her better half. I could feel the beating of her heart.

„Is it true that they are following us?“

„They said they'd give us until the morning to get off the pack lands. We should arrive at the south boundary in an hour in the event that we shift. I'll convey Sasha.“

I heard wolves yelling somewhere out there and the weak cushioning of feet as we approached the line.

„Darling we are nearly there, hang on close.“

Similarly as we arrived at the pack line I heard them behind us, similar to they were attempting effectively to get us rather than simply compelling us across the line. I became diverted and out of nowhere I was tumbling off my dad and into the moist leaves on the ground.

„DADDY!!" I shouted.

„Sasha child! Race to mama!" My mom moved back and raced to me. She pulled me up into her arms and started running once more. I had tumbled off my dad before we arrived at the line. Unexpectedly we were encircled, my dad yelling for his family on the opposite side of the line. My mom attempted to run the extent that she could prior to tossing me hard. I flew through the air as it was penetrated with the shouts of my mom being assaulted and the excruciating yells of my dad who needed to secure me rather than his mate. My dad snatched me and remained past the boundary unfit to do anything. I turned around to see my mom, incapable to get a brief look previously…

My eyes snapped open and I shocked up in my bed. My breathing was shallow and I was canvassed in sweat. I could feel the tears all over and I realized it had been a similar dream I'd had since I was a kid. It generally came up when I was frightened or pushed. It had been some time and I thought I had moved past it. Clearly not.

I checked out my telephone. Six AM. „Beautiful..“ I murmured.

We imagined with regards to mother once more.. I heard Raya whimper.

„I know.“ I could feel the tears stinging my eyes. The night my mom was killed would torment me until the end of time. Despite the fact that my dad never accused me, I accused myself. I took a full breath and a long shower. I took as much time as is needed preparing earlier today, even made myself some genuine breakfast. I was hesitant to return to the workplace. He hadn't terminated me, yet I realized he was searching for an explanation now. I snatched, not really settled to arrive early and have everything set up for the gatherings earlier today.

I strolled into the workplace and was amazed to meet Paul in the entryway.

„Sasha!“ He gave me a comforting grin and a much hotter embrace.

„Paulie!“ I embraced him back firmly.

He ventured back, grasping my shoulders and looking at my face. „It's valid. You've become more lovely since I last saw you."

I scrunched my nose, „Gracious quiet, you enormous tease. You say that to every one of the young ladies!"

He glanced around and murmured, „Not that grouch at gathering. She's a genuine wet blanket." He then, at that point, professed to swoon, „I have an exclusive, keen interest in you, sweetheart."

I giggled, „How have you been, Paul?"

He shrugged, „Standard, worn out, normal, worn out. There was a major panic yesterday so that was invigorating."

„Goodness, I know. Heard with regards to it. I bet you were the one that got it, huh?" I grinned.

„That is no joke'," he pushed my arm prior to accepting me in an embrace once more. „You deal with yourself young lady."

„Continuously. You as well, Paul.“

I advanced up to my work area and plunked down cheerfully. The experience first floor had been actually what I wanted today. Later all of the cruelty of the previous evening I wanted some glow. I went in and set up the meeting room prior to sitting down and really taking a look at the clock. „Eight 45. They'll be here any moment.“

The lift dinged and I saw both of the Thorpes leave.

„Hello, Mr. Thorpe,“ I offered, my voice cold and my once positive state of mind currently gone at seeing that man.

„Miss Lovett,“ he answered prior to entering his office.

Back to the same old thing then, at that point, eh? Raya mumbled and I could feel her feign exacerbation.

„He's simply a bundle of daylight isn't he…“ I answered inside.

„Hello, Miss Lovett!"

I gobbled my head up to see Jim Thorpe. I grinned energetically. „Hello, Beta Jim."

He sat on the edge of my work area and peered down at me with a terrible grin, „Look, I'm grieved with regards to what happened final evening. He reserved no option to blame you without having for current realities."

I shrugged happily, not having any desire to tell him how I truly had an outlook on the circumstance or how furious I really was at his sibling, „It's previously."

He maintained eye contact with me, as though he was looking through my eyes to check whether I was being honest. He fixed and smacked the work area, „Okay, could you let Jackson and I take you to lunch to make it dependent upon you."

I shook my head, there was nothing I'd prefer do less. „You don't need to do that."

„I demand."

„All things considered, I really can't today. Mr Thorpe has a lunch meeting this evening and I will presumably be required too to take notes."

He gestured his head, „Okay, okay… IOU then, at that point."

I grinned. „Not likely," I contemplated internally.

We are NOT going to willfully invest energy with that jerk, Jackson Thorpe! Raya snarled. I could see she was as yet sore with regards to the manner in which our mate had treated us the previous evening. I was indeed pulled from my musings by the telephone ringing.

„Indeed Mr. Price, we totally comprehend. Inform us as to whether there's anything you really want."

I stood and strolled into Mr. Thorpe's office. I was indeed smacked in the face by his fragrance. „Mr Thorpe?" I asked as I entered.

„Well," he muttered from his work area, not in any event, turning upward.

„Your 9am gathering has dropped."

He turned upward, marginally bothered, „Did they give an explanation?"

I stepped in further, „Mr Price's significant other has started giving birth."

He reclined in his seat and scoured his head, „Indeed, I surmise the extent that reasons put in any amount of work of the best. Did they reschedule?"

„Indeed, I put them down for next Wednesday at two. It was the main open space accessible. Assuming that doesn't work I can get back to them."

He shook his head, „No that is fine. I suppose you can go clear up the gathering room and set up for the gathering this evening."

„Indeed, sir," I answered rather briskly, still not prepared to pardon him yet.

„Miss Lovett?"

„Well?" I turned around to confront him, keeping my demeanor even. I needed to holler at him however I realized that would just cause me problems.

He frowned at me, „No doubt about it.."

„All things considered, I don't warmly embrace being blamed for taking dependent on my experience. Excuse me." I turned and left the room, pleased I'd tell him how I felt.

It didn't keep going long however, and I half-staggered back to my work area. It was the most startling and inebriating discussion I'd at any point had. I was as yet disturbed from the previous evening, however the moment I got his fragrance I was demolished. It was a little disturbing how apparently unbothered he was the point at which I was about prepared to one or the other run for the slopes or have sex with him.

„Inhale, Sasha, inhale," I murmured as I remained to go change out the gathering room, actually contemplating whether my mate was even half as impacted by me as I was by him, in any event, when I resented him.

EIGHT

SASHA

Thankfully the rest of the week went off without a hitch. I made it my mission to at least make it a week, just to prove him wrong. He didn't even seem fazed by it but I was proud he hadn't scared me off. I had stuck my ground and yesterday I had gotten my first paycheck. This morning I woke with a spring in my step and I had plans! And when I say plans, I mean apartment hunting and maybe finding some new work clothes. I could not wait to get out of my tiny, dingy apartment on the not-so-great part of town.

Living in Charlotte, North Carolina had so far been the best stop in my wide range of homes. My dad and I had moved around so much, trying to find a safe place for us to stay. We had finally settled in a small beach town in the very southern part of Florida but when he had died I didn't stick around for very long.

After driving around the city, hopefully finding a nicer place that was closer to work I found a few good options. I took part of my paycheck and used it as a deposit on a comfortable loft apartment only a few blocks from work. A solid ten minute walk to the office, three minutes if I was driving. Way better than the almost twenty-minute drive I was currently making. It was a loft in a historic building near downtown and I loved it the minute I walked in. There were large windows and brick accent walls mixed in with the crisp white walls. It had high ceilings and a good sized living area and kitchen. The kitchen had up to date appliances and I was so excited about the dishwasher. I had never had one before. There was one bedroom with its own ensuite bathroom and a walk in closet. I moved in next weekend and decided to spend the rest of the weekend packing my things.

Monday morning came all too quickly and I found myself dreading going into the office. I was still tender about being accused for stealing those files but I had decided I was going to try and move past it.

"Good morning, Mr. Thorpe."

"Good morning, Miss Lovett. My office please."

I followed him in and watched as he removed his suit coat and hung it up, his muscular arms stretching the fabric of his shirt as he lifted them. I could hear Raya groan in my head. He was a jerk but I couldn't deny he was one attractive man. Jackson was tall and fit. He wasn't huge like guys you see at the gym who lift and lift until every muscle is bulging in gross ways. He was lean and muscular. His jawline could cut glass and his dark hair was high and tight, curling a bit at the top and making me want to run my hands through it. I looked up to see his bright blue eyes on me and I knew I had been caught staring.

"What can I help you with, Mr. Thorpe?"

"Do you have the files I asked for in my email this morning?"

"Yes," I replied setting them down on his desk. "There's also a revised plan for the meeting next week."

"Thank you."

"Anything else?"

"That's it for now."

I smiled and left the room, I sat down at my desk and I could feel how drained my energy was. "Coffee.. I need coffee," I mumbled. I stood and made my way to the break room and made myself a cup, hesitating for a moment before deciding to be nice and make one for Jackson as well. Just because he was a jerk didn't mean I needed to be.

"Mr. Thorpe?"

"Yes?" he looked up from his desk and I attempted to give a warm smile.

"I felt myself dragging a bit and thought you might need a pick me up as well. Coffee?" I offered the cup and he let out a sigh.

"Please. I guess what they say about Mondays is true," he replied, taking the cup from me. Our fingers brushed and the spark it sent through my body was enough to keep me going the rest of the day. I was sure he felt it too, but once again he seemed indifferent as he looked back down at his work.

"Thank you, Miss Lovett."

I managed a smile before walking out and practically collapsing at my desk.

Ding!

I looked at the message on my computer.

My office.

I rolled my eyes and with a sigh walked back to his office.

"Yes, Mr. Thorpe?"

"Miss Lovett, did you check these before giving them to me?"

"I'm not sure what you mean," I replied, confused as to what he was now saying I had done wrong. Again.

"Did you check these before giving them to me, yes or no?"

"Of course I did. Is there something wrong?"

"Well, maybe the fact that none of them are the files I actually asked for?"

I exhaled, "I'm sorry sir. I must have grabbed the wrong pile." I walked back out to my desk and sure enough was the pile of files he had asked for. "I'm sorry."

"Don't be sorry just do the job. Waste of time..." he mumbled as he took the files from me.

I grabbed the wrong files off his desk and turned with a huff back out to my desk.

Can we kill him yet? Raya smirked in my head and it made me laugh. She used to ask me that daily when we worked for Mr. Bettany.

"I thought you were in love? Something about him being our mate?" I replied. She grumbled and I laughed again before continuing with my work.

The day began to drag on as it came to its close and I just about jumped out of my chair when that clock turned to five.

"Mr. Thorpe?" I asked as I tapped on the door.

"Hmm?" I heard him hum at me but he wasn't at his desk. I looked around the room and I saw him lying on the couch to the side, his sleeves rolled up and hand resting on his head.

I walked over to him, trying to hide the worry in my voice. "Are you okay?"

He attempted to wave me off, "It's just a headache, nothing major. Have a good night, Miss Lovett."

I walked out of the room and back in with a handful of pills. I poured a glass of water from the cart and took it to him, sitting on the coffee table across from the sofa. I leaned in and offered my hand filled with pills. "Here."

He looked up at me, "I'm fine."

"Don't be stubborn, just take the pills. They'll help."

He gave me a frown before taking the medicine from my hand and the water. "Thank you," he said as he laid back down with his eyes closed.

"You're welcome," I replied, trying not to let it go to my head. "Do you want me to get you anything? I can order you something to eat or have a car called so you don't have to drive home."

He looked up at me, his face tight, "Why are you being so nice?"

I straightened myself, "I'm always this nice Mr. Thorpe, you just haven't let me be this nice."

He scoffed and closed his eyes again, "Yeah, sure."

I let out a sigh, not wanting to start an argument with this man at this moment. "Are you feeling better?"

He nodded his head, "A little, thank you."

"Then goodnight, Mr. Thorpe," I spoke flatly in an attempt to hide my mild irritation. I stood and began to walk toward the door when I felt him behind me.

"Sasha."

I turned around and looked up, meeting his eyes. "Yes, Mr. Thorpe?"

Suddenly I was pulled in to him, his arms woven around my waist. My hands instantly shot up, resting between his chest and mine and I could feel his warmth through the thin fabric of his shirt as my hand brushed his chest. His lips came crashing down to mine and I was enveloped in a passionate kiss. My whole body was telling me yes. This was my mate and I wanted him. I kissed him back but only for a moment before my mind caught up to me. This guy was a jerk. He had falsly accused me of espionage. He had belittled me and at times even terrified me. He had treated me rather horribly for almost two weeks, why was I falling into him like he deserved my affection? I could feel the anger swelling in me.

I pushed him off, shooting myself backward. I breathed deeply and slapped him hard across the face. I could feel the tears welling in my eyes but he was not about to see me cry, so I turned and rushed out of the office.

NINE

SASHA

I walked into the office the next morning, extremely glad it was Tuesday and I wouldn't be seeing him at all today. I sat at my desk, working hard to get as much done as I could before lunch when I heard a familiar 'ding'.

Miss Lovett,

I left a few pack files I need for today on my desk. Can you please grab them and bring them to me at the pack house? I will send you the address.

Jackson Thorpe

There went my good mood. I couldn't breathe. Literally. Did he forget who I was?! There was no way I was stepping foot onto a pack's territory. I was a rogue! I was already pushing it working here. I took a deep breath and replied.

Mr. Thorpe,

I'm sorry but I can't leave the office unattended. Can you possibly send a pack member for the files? I will have them sealed and ready to go.

S. Lovett

"Please let that work," I whispered as I sent it.

No. I've texted you the address. Be here in an hour.

I don't even remember walking to my car or even arriving at his pack boundary. I sat at an idle outside the gate of the pack territory, frozen in fear. The last time I had attempted to enter another pack's territory I had almost been killed. I looked at the clock, I had twenty minutes to make it to the pack house. I took a deep breath and drove down the long driveway.

After about ten minutes I made it to the pack house. It was a beautiful building. Two stories with white paneling and large windows. There was a large porch in the front that wrapped around the sides. I stopped in front of the house. I could feel myself panicking. My breaths were uneven at best and my heart was going a million beats a minute. I stepped out of the car and walked up the porch and to the door on shaky legs. I rang the bell and a woman answered with a smile before she smelled me and her whole face changed and she scowled at me. She knew what I was.

"What do you want?" she spat.

"I'm Sasha Lovett, Mr. Thorpe's PA. I have some files he requested," I replied quietly.

"Hmm." She stepped aside and let me enter. "Stay here, I'll go get him."

She didn't have to worry, I wasn't going anywhere. I'm pretty sure my legs had stopped working. I was one strong breeze away from falling over.

"Miss Lovett, thank you for bringing those." My eyes shot up at the familiar voice to meet the eyes of Jackson. His eyes darkened when he saw the apparent look of fear in my face. There was no way I could hide it.

"Sasha, you're shaking. What happened?"

Breathe love, our mate won't hurt us.. Raya spoke in my mind.

I took a breath, "I- umm... nothing. Here's your files." I practically threw them at him before turning away. "I'll see you tomorrow."

"Stay for lunch, it's the least I can do for making you drive out here during your lunch hour," he offered, sounding much more relaxed being at home.

"It's no problem, I'll just grab something on the way back. Bye," I replied quickly, trying to get myself out of there as fast as possible.

Suddenly my arm was being grabbed and I let out an involuntary yelp as I was pulled through the house and into an office.

"Sit."

I was placed in a chair and he sat across from me, his face stern.

"Sasha, what is wrong?"

"I just need to get back to work that's all."

"Sasha I'm an Alpha, I can tell you're lying."

I stopped for a minute, "I'm pretty sure you can't."

"I still know that you're lying. When you looked at me a few minutes ago I saw real fear. Why? Did someone hurt you?"

I shook my head, "I just don't like packs..."

His eyes widened, realizing what he had done. "I- I'm so sorry. I didn't think this would be an issue since you work at the company. Sasha, I wouldn't allow anyone in this pack to hurt you."

"I should go," I replied. I didn't care what he said, I wasn't going to stay here any longer. I didn't belong here. I stood to go and he grabbed my hand, pulling me closer to him but not quite touching.

"Sasha, I need you to hear me. Nobody is going to hurt you."

I shook my head, "I can't afford to believe you, Jackson. I- I learned my lesson about walking onto pack lands. There's a reason I didn't want to come here. But you insisted."

"Sasha, I-"

"No. I can't be here. You want to know what happened the last time I walked through a pack boundary?" I lifted my shirt, exposing my abdomen and the scar that went down my ribcage from just beneath my breast to my hip. "My dad had just died and I was 16, homeless, and had nothing. I wandered onto a pack's territory in search of shelter and food, hoping since I was a kid they would take pity on me. Instead they attempted to slice me up into pieces. I didn't have my wolf yet. I almost died." I lowered my shirt again and I could feel the tears as they began dripping down my cheeks. "THAT is what happens when you enter a pack territory."

Jackson just stared at me, the shock in his face was deep and painful. I let out a long exhale, "I can't be here. I don't belong here. I just..."

"I understand," he said quietly. I snapped my head up, my eyes meeting his. "Sasha, I had no idea. I'm sorry. I'll drive you home."

I shook my head, "I drove myself, that would be silly."

"Then let me at least ride with you to the edge of the border," he asked and I had to admit it made me feel better.

I nodded with a faint smile and we walked out to my car. It was old and beaten up but it worked. "This is your car?" he asked in disbelief.

"Orphan, remember?"

He nodded and rode with me to the border. I stopped at the gate and turned to him, "Thank you for staying with me. I know I was a bit of a mess."

Jackson just gave a tight smile before climbing out of the car. "See you tomorrow."

"Bye," I smiled as I drove back to the office.

TEN

JACKSON

As I walked back down the long driveway to the pack house I couldn't wrap my head around it. The intense fear she'd had just driving onto our territory. Our pack had its fair share of rogue encounters but they were always violent. He couldn't imagine what would possess a pack to attack a teenager who wasn't even able to shift yet. That would have never been okay here.

Something had shifted in me and I could feel it. Suddenly I wanted to know everything about her. How was the strong, caring, kind, fiery woman from last night the same person as the terrified, shaking, neglected girl that I had just witnessed.

"Jimmy," I threw out in the mind link.

"Yep?"

"I want you to find out everything you can about Sasha."

"Seriously? You want me to do a background check on your mate?" I could hear the attitude from miles away. "Jack, why don't you do something real crazy and just talk to her? Ask her yourself?"

"Jimmy, just do it."

He grumbled something that I'm sure was inappropriate before severing the link. I didn't know what he was going to find but I needed to know more. Most rogues became that way by choice, because they challenged an Alpha or broke a pack law. Most rogues were mangey and animalistic, practically losing touch with their human side. But Sasha was different, almost as if she had been forced into this.

My mind was taken back to earlier today. I had fought every cell in my body telling me to hold her. Even though she had an affect on me she was still a rogue and I couldn't let her in unless I knew what had made her that way. I had a pack to protect. I couldn't just let a rogue into the pack without making sure they wouldn't endanger my people, whether or not they were my mate. But the way her long blonde hair flowed in waves down her back, the way her petite frame was somehow fit and tight but curvy at the same time. Her deep chocolate eyes looking up at me and almost relieved when she saw me in the entrance of the pack house just about had me ruined right then and there.

I shook my head, "Stop."

Why didn't we go with our mate? She's clearly upset. You're an idiot... Blaize whined.

"We have an entire pack to think about. I can't let her in before I'm sure she won't bring harm to any of the people I've sworn to protect. You know that," I mumbled. "We've come too far to endanger our people. It took us a long time to gain their trust after the abuse they suffered at the hands of our father. We can't just bring a rogue in without being positive."

Blaize growled softly, he obviously didn't like my answer but knew I was a little bit right.

The next morning Jimmy mind linked me that he needed me first thing before I left.

"What's up Jim?" I asked as I walked into his office at the pack house.

"I looked her up like you wanted."

"And?" I asked, my interest fully piqued.

"And there isn't much to say."

"What do you mean?" I frowned.

"I could barely find anything. I even had one of our guys help look into other packs to see where she came from. We searched up and down the East Coast as well as further inland and couldn't find her anywhere. Either someone erased their information or Sasha Lovett isn't her real name."

I scowled, that was not the answer I wanted. "Guess I'll have to do some digging. Thanks, Jimmy."

"You know Jackson, you could just get to know her."

I rolled my eyes. "Yeah, yeah, thanks for your sage advice, Jim," I grumbled before making my way to work.

ELEVEN

SASHA

"We WILL have a good day," I whispered to myself as I sat at my desk the next morning. Yesterday, having to go out to the pack house had really done a number on me. I was surprised when Jackson had been so kind.

He was a bit out of character yesterday, Raya said as she heard me thinking about Jackson.

"Maybe that is his character. Jim said he was the best Alpha they've had in a long time. Maybe it's just because I'm a rogue." I could feel Raya shrug. I knew she hated being a rogue. Wolves are meant to have a pack and she had put too much stock on finding a mate that would let us into a pack. Although I wasn't as sure that he would reject me now, I also wasn't sure he would keep me.

"Good morning, Miss Lovett."

"Good morning, Mr. Thorpe," I smiled as he walked past and into his office.

Miss Lovett,

I have conference calls all morning. Please make sure I'm not disturbed.

Jackson

I nodded to myself and continued with my work. I knew conference calls were the worst and I wanted to give a small thank you for being so understanding about yesterday so I made a hot pot of coffee and put it in a thermal pot so it would stay warm for him. I took it and a cup and walked into his office slowly. He looked up at me as I walked in, still in the middle of a call. I gave a small smile before setting the pot down on the coffee table and pouring a cup. I took it to his desk and set it down gently before walking out of the office and back to my desk.

I know how long back to back conference calls can be. Hope the coffee helps, let me know if you need anything else and I'll bring it to you.

S. Lovett

My message went unanswered like I expected it would. A few hours later he emerged from his office as I was standing to go to lunch. I was excited to be starting back up with my Wednesday lunch dates with Paul.

"Thank you for the coffee, it definitely helped." He eyed me as I stood up, "Headed out to lunch?"

"Kind of. I have a lunch date," I said with a smile and a smirk.

Jackson's whole face changed to a scowl, "Enjoy your lunch." With that he sulked back into his office.

It would have been kind of me to mention it was with the sixty year old Paul but that wouldn't have been as fun. I took the elevator down to the lobby and Paul and I sat on a bench just outside the building.

"How's my girl doing?" he asked as I picked at my lunch.

"I'm alright. It's been a stressful couple of days but I think it's looking up."

"That's good," he smiled, squeezing my hand.

"How is the security room?" I questioned.

"Eh. Pretty much watching TV all day, who can complain right? It's amazing what people do when they think nobody is watching."

Sasha laughed, "Okay so how many nose pickers and makeout sessions have you caught?"

"Too many..." He shook his head with a laugh. "Is that boss of ours treating you well, Miss PA?"

"He's a bit difficult at times but I think he's warming up to me," I said with a shrug.

"He'd have to be a fool not to."

I made my way back up from lunch to find Jackson standing at my desk.

"Mr. Thorpe, can I help you?"

"You're five minutes late from lunch," he growled.

I rolled my eyes, "I'm sorry, sir. It won't happen again."

"Must have had too much fun on your date."

"I did," I replied, sass dripping from my words. I was going to be nice and tell him about Paul, but not now. Now I was going to just let him stew.

He stomped back to his office and I knew I hadn't heard the last of it. Sure enough, five minutes later I heard the ding.

Miss Lovett, my office.

I fully regret my decision teasing him.

"Yes, Mr. Thorpe?" I asked as I entered.

"Do you enjoy teasing your boss?"

"I'm not sure what you mean, sir," I replied with a shrug. I smacked myself internally. Stop it Sasha! Why couldn't I turn off the sass?

I looked up to see his eyes burning, "Your hot date with Paul?"

"I would have used 'enjoyable' to describe it personally." Now I was going too far. He was going to snap me in half.

Jackson stood and rounded his desk, bounding towards me. I backed up, only for my back to meet the door. "You are my mate, you do not date other men."

It was my turn to have fury in my eyes, "No I'm not, because if we were mates you would take care of me and love me not push me around like some mangey pup."

He stepped back surprised at my response before leaning forward again. "You will not see him again."

"Oh, yes I will!" I scoffed. "I'll see him next Wednesday and the Wednesday after that and the Wednesday after that for however long I like!" I glared at him. It had gone from a game to a fight as he became almost possessive.

"Sasha." He let out a deep breath before speaking again, "I can't have you with other men. I'll go crazy."

It was my turn to be shocked. I couldn't find the words to reply to him.

TWELVE

SASHA

What does he mean he'll go crazy? He's been here acting like his mate bond is practically nonexistent. Hot and cold couldn't even begin to describe how this man was acting.

I knew if I stayed in there any longer he would probably try something like the other day. I wasn't about to just be his little rogue toy. I let out a small huff and left his office. After receiving a call from reception that his one o'clock meeting was here I sent him a message.

Mr. Thorpe,

Your 1pm meeting is early. Shall I send them in when they come up?

He didn't reply which was irritating. I would just have them wait for a moment I guess. Off the elevator bounded a tall, bright woman. To my surprise, she was met by Beta Jim who gave her a hug and they walked arm in arm past me and into Jackson's office.

"Apparently it's an informal meeting," I mumbled and started back on some files I had been working on. I could hear laughing and talking through the thin walls and after an hour they all exited the office.

"Oh Miss Lovett, let me introduce you to someone," Jim hollered as they walked toward my desk. "This is our mother, Amalia."

I stood with a smile and offered my hand, "I'm pleased to meet you, Mrs. Thorpe."

"Oh please, call me Amalia dear," she smiled. As she held my hand I could feel warmth radiating off of her. It filled my whole center, releasing a calm over me. She placed her other hand on top of mine and gave me a sad smile, "Sweetheart, you have been through so much."

I pulled my hand back, confused at what had just happened. "I..."

"I'm sorry Miss Lovett, I have a hard time turning it off sometimes," she gave an apologetic smile. I was still confused.

"Mom is a healer," Jim explained. "She can feel others' emotions and calm them, or heal those who are injured." My eyes widened, I had heard of them but never actually met one.

"I didn't mean to pry," she smiled, "I could feel the pain rolling off you the moment I touched your hand."

I shook my head, "No, I-"

"Don't be embarrassed, we all have a past," she smiled warmly and began walking toward the elevator. "I'm glad to meet you dear."

I didn't quite know what to say. I looked up to see Jackson staring at me. His eyes held questions. Questions I wasn't about to answer.

"Do you need anything else, Mr. Thorpe?"

He shook his head.

"Okay then, I'm going to take my lunch." With that I grabbed my phone and rushed to the break room.

I sat down at the table with my head in my hands as I played with the bag of tea in my mug.

"What did she mean?"

My head snapped up at the voice to see Jackson leaning against the doorway. I shook my head, "It was nothing."

"My mom is never wrong. What happened to you, Sasha?"

I let out a nervous laugh, "That's a long story."

"Well, we have time," he offered, sitting down next to me.

"A long story I'd rather not get into at the moment," I replied, turning back to my tea.

He nodded, "That's fine." He got up and for a moment I thought he was leaving but he walked around me and into the kitchen, grabbing some boxed lunches from the fridge.

"Eat," he said as he placed a box in front of me before sitting down beside me with his own.

I looked up at him with a bit of a confused look, "Why are you being so nice to me?"

He smiled and threw my own words back at me, "I'm always this nice, Miss Lovett. You just haven't let me be nice."

I shook my head. "Yeah, sure," I mumbled.

"Plans for the weekend?"

I shrugged, "Not really. I'm moving, which I'm excited about."

His head bolted up, "Moving?"

"Yep, I found a nice loft at a really good price a few blocks from here."

"Where are you now?"

"Not in a really nice loft..." I muttered.

I could feel his scowl from here. I was not giving him the information he wanted. We ate in silence, not really knowing what to say to each other.

"Well," I said as I got up, taking my lunch to the garbage. "Thank you for sitting with me. I should get back to work."

He nodded, "We only have a few more things to do today. You can head home when we're done."

"Really?" I turned to him surprised, I hadn't had an early day in, well, ever.

"Really." He turned to me, "You did a good job the last two weeks, I thought for sure you would have quit by the end of the first week."

I chuckled, "Oh, it definitely crossed my mind." We walked back down the hallway together and I sat at my desk. He stood above me quietly. I looked up at him, "Yes?"

He grumbled something incoherent and walked into his office. "Okay then," I whispered before finishing up the last of my paperwork.

I've finished all I needed to, do you need anything else today?

Sasha

I began gathering my things, hoping he wasn't going to take back his offer to let me off early.

Yes, please come to my office.

I groaned, I knew that was too good to be true. I walked in and up to his desk.

"Sit, Miss Lovett."

I sat down and he met my eyes. "Is there a way I can convince you to come back to the pack house on Tuesday?"

I recoiled. "I.. I don't know.."

"Miss Lovett, I understand your past with packs is shaky at best. But you have my word nobody in my pack will treat you that way. You will be safe."

"Mr. Thorpe..."

"As my PA I will need you occasionally at the pack house to do some work. Is this going to be a problem?"

I lowered my head, I knew he was right. "No, sir."

I looked up when he didn't reply and he was smiling. "Good, you can go now. I'll see you Monday."

I stood up, trying not to freak out on my way out. I knew it was going to suck going back there.

Our mate will keep us safe. He promised, you heard him.

"We'll see..." I mumbled as I made it to my car and drove home. The rest of the evening was spent cleaning up the apartment. I didn't own much, so tomorrow would be an easy move. I had an old couch and an old mattress on a metal frame. Those were the only large items. Hopefully after saving up I could buy myself some new furniture. Other than that it was just a collection of boxes filled with the small amount of belongings I'd collected over the years.

It neared midnight and I stood in my spotless apartment with my hands on my hips. A smile spread on my face at the thought that tomorrow night I would be sleeping in my new place.

THIRTEEN

JACKSON

I may or may not have looked up her employee info last night. I know it was against the rules, but do those rules really apply to mates? I leaned against my pickup truck outside her building, sipping my coffee. I had gotten here early and when I saw where she had been living I needed to take a minute to calm down. This place was a hole.

"Jackson?"

I looked up from my thoughts to see Sasha standing in front of me carrying a box. "Hey."

"What are you doing here?"

"You mentioned you were moving, I thought I'd give you a hand."

"You really don't need to do that." She walked past me and to her janky car, placing the box in the trunk.

"You were planning on moving a couch by yourself?"

She smirked, "How do you think I got it inside in the first place?"

My eyes widened. "Touché. Well anyway, I'm here. I might as well help."

She shrugged before opening the door to the building, "Might as well."

I followed her up, my eyes wide as I looked around. How was it possible it actually looked worse on the inside? We stepped into her tiny apartment and I tried to contain my disappointment. How had she lived here? No wolf should be contained like this. I grabbed one end of the old used couch and helped her carry it to my truck, followed by her bed and the small amount of boxes.

"That it?" I clapped my hands together as we placed the final boxes in my truck.

"Yep. Let me hand over my keys and I'll meet you back here in five."

I climbed in the truck and sat back in my seat. "Mom was right, what is this girl going through?"

I saw her walk to her car with a wave. I followed her through town, stopping in front of a nice building. "Thank goodness," I mumbled. We each grabbed a few boxes and I followed her up.

"Nice place," I offered as we walked in to her loft.

"Thanks! Definitely a step up from the pit I was living in before."

"I wasn't going to say anything..." I rubbed my head innocently as I set the boxes on the floor. She gave me a warm smile and we quickly finished bringing up all her things.

Sasha sat down on her couch with a sigh. "Well I'm going to order some pizza, want to join me?"

"Sure," I shrugged, sitting down on the couch next to her. I leaned my head back and closed my eyes for a minute while she ordered

"It will be about twenty five minutes. You can relax for a bit, I'm going to try and find the boxes for the kitchen."

I got up and sat at one of the stools at the island, "I can help."

"Don't worry about it, I mostly just need to find the cups," she laughed as she started sifting through boxes.

I watched her as she moved around the apartment. She swayed and smiled. I hadn't seen her happy since I'd met her almost three weeks ago. Watching her was intoxicating. My thoughts were interrupted by the sound of the door.

"Pizza is here!" She smiled, holding two boxes of pizza and some sodas. We sat at the kitchen island, eating and talking lightly.

"Sasha, how did you become a rogue?"

She snapped her head up to face me and I could tell she was trying to decide if she should tell me. She looked down and took a deep breath. This was it, I was finally learning about this mystery mate of mine.

"My family was exiled when I was four."

I could feel the shock spread across my face. She had been a rogue her whole life.

"I didn't know why we had left our pack, I was too young to understand. But when I grew up my dad my told me. The pack we were in, the Alpha had become abusive. He would beat the pack members into submission and ruled by fear and violence. My father caught him beating a pup and ended up challenging him. He didn't like that and instead of performing the challenge like the law required he exiled my family, threatening to kill all of us if we didn't leave. I don't remember where it was or even the name of the pack. My dad never told me and I don't have any memories I can remember of that time. The last thing I remember was the night we left, being chased through the woods to the pack border."

I didn't know what to say. I had lost all words. What her family had gone through, it was horrible. "Sasha, I'm so sorry. I had no idea."

She smiled, "Nobody does. When you think of rogues you think of criminals who deserved their exile or rebels who didn't want to follow the laws of the pack. You don't think of a family just trying to protect themselves."

"You've been a rogue your whole life.."

"Pretty much. My dad and I moved around a lot in the search for a safe place to live. We finally found a place down in a small town in Florida, but when he died I had nowhere to go so I moved around some more before finding my way here."

"Your dad? What about your mom?"

She turned away and I could tell she was upset, "She umm... she was killed that night."

I let out a small gasp by accident and she turned to me. I could see the tears in her eyes fighting to fall.

"It was my fault, I had fallen when we were just shy of the border. She ran to me and was only able to throw me to safety before they found us and attacked her. My father never fully recovered from losing her."

I turned to her, pulling her stool closer to me so she was sitting between my legs. I pulled her into me. I knew I'd regret it later, I could feel myself wanting her more and more. I needed to know more though, still not knowing if she would end up endangering my pack. Even though she seemed kind, rogues were a bit questionable. But in this moment I felt sorry, and I knew she was hurting. She broke down in my arms, releasing what I'm sure was years of unshed tears and pain. After a while her sobs slowed and she pushed away from me.

"Gosh, you must think I'm a mess," she said as she wiped away the remaining tears from her face.

"Actually I think you're strong," I replied, giving her a smile.

She took a deep breath and turned away, hiding the blush in her cheeks I had caught a glimpse of. "Well thanks for today. It was nice having help."

I took the hint. She wanted to play in her new apartment. "I should head back, lots of work to do back at the pack."

I walked to the door and turned to her. Before my mind knew what I was doing my body rebeled and I found myself leaning down and placing a kiss on her cheek. She blushed again which stirred me. I wanted more.

But instead I walked out the door. "Goodnight, Miss Lovett."

"Goodnight, Mr. Thorpe."

FOURTEEN

SASHA

My hand touched my cheek as I closed the door. Today had been different. He had been different. I could feel myself beginning to open up to Jackson and it terrified me. He had made it clear he didn't want a rogue as a mate, that I was a risk to him and his people. But at the same time he had been so kind.

"He is probably just a good guy. Didn't know how to respond to some girl crying at him," I muttered as I walked back inside, earning a growl from Raya. I smiled as I entered the loft. I was in love with this place. I spent the rest of the night unpacking and setting up my new home. The rest of the weekend was spent sleeping and watching movies, comfortable and feeling safe in my new home.

"Good morning, Miss Lovett."

I looked up at the familiar voice and smiled, "Good morning, Mr. Thorpe."

"Good weekend?" He asked as he passed through to his office.

"Good, relaxing," I replied following him in. "Thanks again for helping on Saturday. How was the rest of your weekend?"

He shrugged, "It was alright."

I looked down at my paper, "So this morning you have a conference call with Reeds Tech at ten. Then you're open until your meeting across town at three."

"Sounds good. Would you mind ordering in some lunch? Have it dropped at noon."

"Will do," I smiled and walked out of the room. I sat at my desk and exhaled. He smelled so good. His scent had been teasing me the entire conversation and I was about to lose it. Was I really the only one having a hard time like this?

Just before noon his lunch was delivered and I took the bag in. "Lunch is served," I said, raising the bag in the air.

He sat up and walked toward me. "Good, I'm starving."

He sat on the couch and I handed him the bag before turning to leave, "Enjoy."

"Wait, you're not joining me?"

I looked back at him and he seemed almost disappointed. "You want me to sit there and watch you eat lunch?"

He gave me a puzzled look before looking in the bag, "Why didn't you grab yourself something?"

I shrugged, "I didn't know I could. I thought you meant lunch for yourself."

Jackson rolled his eyes before walking out of the office and coming back with a box lunch from the fridge. He opened all of the food and then split it all between two plates.

"There. Come eat."

I smiled, enjoying the fact he was trying so hard to spend some time with me as I sat beside him.

Mate wants us, Raya whispered.

"He's just being nice," I replied.

No. You're just being stubborn. He wants us.

"We'll see," I mumbled internally.

He took a few bites of his food before sitting back, "So in terms of tomorrow..."

I could feel myself tense. I had forgotten he had asked me to come to the pack house to work tomorrow. "Uh.. yeah. Tomorrow."

I felt a hand on my shoulder, "Sasha, I promise it will be okay. In all honesty, it will actually be a pretty boring day."

I gave him a smile but I was still hesitant. I couldn't just erase twenty years of experiences being a rogue. There was a lot I had seen.

I stood in front of the pack house again. This time to spend the whole day, not a mere few minutes. I could feel myself shaking and on the verge of hyperventillating. I was still terrified, even if Jackson said nobody would hurt me, it wasn't something I was going to get over after one visit.

Breathe... Raya whispered. *We will make it through today. We can't be terrified of this place forever.*

I nodded. My wolf was right. I walked up the steps and was about to knock on the door when it swung open. I'd be lying if I said I didn't flinch.

"Miss Lovett! Oh, I'm so glad you're here!" Jackson's mother Amalia smiled warmly before placing her arm around my shoulders and walking me into the house. I knew why she was doing it, I could feel myself calming down as we walked.

"Please, call me Sasha," I offered with a smile.

"Okay Sasha, I know you have a lot to be afraid of dear, but this house isn't one of them. And if anyone says otherwise you send them to me." She gave me a wink and a squeeze before letting me go and knocking on a door. "Head on in hun, he's waiting for you."

I walked in the room and was immediately overwhelmed by sage and bergamot. "Jackson," I whispered to myself. I stepped further into the room and spoke, "Good morning, Mr. Thorpe."

He looked up from his papers and gave me a smile, "You made it."

"I made it," I countered with a small shrug.

"Take a seat, let me finish this up and I'll let you know what I need you to do."

I gave a nod and then sat in a chair across from his desk. I looked around the room while I waited. It was definitely the office of an Alpha. It almost screamed masculinity. Everything was wood and leather and metal. I turned back to Jackson, watching him as he worked. His hair was messed from running his hands through it too many times. He was dressed in a button down shirt and slacks instead of his usual dark suit and I enjoyed seeing the short sleeves trying to win a fight against his bulging muscles.

My thoughts were cut short by his warm tone. "Alright, all done."

I met his eyes with a small smile, still nervous of my surroundings. Being near him definitely helped my anxiety. "Okay, what do you need me to do?"

"I'll show you." He stood and opened a door to his left. I walked over and my eyes widened at the chaos in the room. Files. Everywhere.

"Oh dear..." I sighed.

Jackson rubbed the back of his head, "Yeah. It's become a bit of a mess. Can you help?"

"I'll try." I shook my head in disbelief before throwing my hair up into a messy bun and walking into the small room. "I'm probably going to need an insane amount of coffee."

"Yes ma'am," he smirked and walked out of his office. I began to work, taking stacks of files and placing them in piles. Jackson walked back in with a cart of assorted drinks and snacks.

"I figured we'd just need all of this."

"Smart," I laughed as I gazed at the cart full of food and caffeine.

After a few hours I grabbed the last of the files and placed them on his desk. "Okay, almost done. I don't quite know what these files are for or what they are about so I need you to tell me where to put them."

Jackson looked through each file and gave them back to me so I could place them in their proper spots. I stood outside the closet, my hands on my hips, "Okay! Done."

Jackson looked up from his work and walked over to the very organized closet. "Awesome! I have a few more things I need your help with that we can go over after lunch. Hungry?"

The growl in my stomach answered his question and he gave me a wink before leading me out of the office.

FIFTEEN

SASHA

"This is the pack kitchen," he explained as we walked through to the common area. "Anyone who wants to come eat here is welcome. We feed anywhere from fifteen to thirty people per meal."

"That's amazing," I replied, taking in the house. It was bright and inviting in the pack house and I could see the appeal.

"All done with work?" Amalia hollered as we entered the pack kitchen and dining hall.

"For now, we've got a bit more to do after lunch." Jackson smiled brightly at his mother and I could tell he was comfortable here.

As pack members started trickling in for lunch I could feel my anxiety creeping back. I could feel their eyes on me, they knew I wasn't part of their pack. It was easy to sniff out a rogue. As if sensing my fear Jackson gave me a reassuring smile, "Remember, nobody will hurt you in this pack."

I gave him a half-hearted smile as he handed me a plate and we walked to one of the large tables. I was grateful that they all pretty much ignored me until a woman walked up to us with a big belly and a smile. "Jack, is this your new PA?" She sang sweetly, sitting down haphazardly onto the bench.

Jackson stood quickly grabbing her hand, "Gosh Ash, careful!" He helped her onto the bench and I glanced at him sideways. Who the hell was this man I was seeing? Because it wasn't the guy who almost rejected me, or scared me, or yelled at me.

"I'm Ashley, Jim's mate." I was brought back by her sweet tone and a soft handshake.

"Hi, I'm Sasha. When are you due?" I asked, eyeing her very swollen belly.

"Any day now. So excited to no longer resemble some beached mammal," she replied sarcastically. "Wow, Jim said you were pretty but that was an understatement for sure. Sasha, you're gorgeous." She turned her gaze up to Jackson, "How the hell did this grump end up getting such a wonderful girl?"

I could see Jackson roll his eyes. Apparently she knew we were mates and wasn't supposed to say anything. I laughed, "I don't think he knows either? Probably why he fights it so much." I gave him a good long smirk, hoping he'd know I was teasing. I could see his gaze darken a bit before his mother burst into laughter.

"We are going to have SO much fun with this one!" she cried.

"If I had known it meant being outnumbered by you lot I would have rejected her on the spot," he mumbled.

Amalia straightened up and smacked the back of her son's head. "You take that back, Jackson Thorpe."

"Ouch! Mom, I was joking," he rubbed his head, "You do know you can't be smacking around the Alpha right?" The look she gave him could turn a man to stone. "Okay, I take it back."

I attempted to stifle a laugh but was unsuccessful. I quickly bit my lip when his head snapped to me, his gaze full of irritation and something else I couldn't quite place.

Ashley laughed at her brother-in-law, "Lighten up Jack, we were just teasing you. Someone has to keep you grounded. Can't be letting your Alpha get a big head now, can we?"

Jackson rolled his eyes. "Okay. If you're finished corrupting my PA, we have work to get back to." He stood and that was my cue to bid the ladies goodbye and follow him back to the office.

He closed the door to the office and stood close to me. I could feel his breath. "Didn't I tell you something about teasing your boss?" he whispered.

I inhaled sharply, "I..."

I was interrupted when his lips crashed into mine. He wound his arms around me, pulling my body close to his. I kissed him back, knowing I shouldn't, but my mate bond had made it impossible to resist. I wanted him. His lips pressed to mine sending shockwaves through my whole body and I could feel myself melt into him. I wrapped my arms around his neck and my hands tangled in his hair. My lips parted and his tongue made his way in to taste mine. His hands traveled down from my waist to below my hips. He picked me up, my legs wrapping around his waist as he pushed me against the wall, kissing a trail down my jaw to my neck. I let out a quiet moan as he sucked on place just above my collarbone where my mark should be. I could feel his desire for me bulging through his pants and I could feel my own arousal stirring. Then suddenly I was brought back. I was not going to sleep with him just because he had been nice for a few days. I could feel Raya whine in my head when I pushed off from him, stopping our moment. He placed his forehead on mine and searched my eyes before placing a gentle kiss on my cheek. He took a deep breath and walked to his desk. I exhaled, my breath still ragged from our intimate few minutes and I sat down in the chair across from his desk.

He ran his hand through his hair, "So.."

I smiled, "What's next on the agenda, Mr. Thorpe?"

He looked up at me and I could see the desire in his eyes before lowering his gaze. "We have a big monthly pack meeting coming up. We have a meeting every week but once a month we make it a big deal- dinner, dancing, games for the kids. It's this Friday and time got away from me. Would you mind helping me get everything planned? I'm the worst at planning parties."

I smiled warmly at him, "Of course. How many people?"

"There will be two hundred attending."

I wrote down notes as we continued talking about food, music, games, who to call for set up and catering.

I gave him the list I had made when we were finished, "Okay, here it all is. Give these numbers to your food people and put someone in charge of setting up and supervising the games for the kids. Do you want me to send out an email reminder?"

"That would be great actually."

I gave him a smile before grabbing my laptop out of my bag and sending one out real quick to the pack. "Done."

Jackson leaned back in his chair and gave me a smile, "Thank you for your help today. I know how hard it was for you to come here."

"I'm glad I did. I can't be scared of this place forever right?" I had to admit I was feeling better. The day had gone so well and I had become a bit more comfortable. "It'll take some time, but I'm warming up to it."

I gathered my things and he walked me out. As we reached my car he took my hands in his, holding them tightly but gentle. He looked down to me, his voice quiet, "Thank you, Sasha."

I looked up at him, meeting his deep, crisp blue eyes. "You're welcome, Jackson." I gave him a smile and squeezed his hand before letting go and climbing in the car, hoping he couldn't hear the massive pounding of my heart.

SIXTEEN

JACKSON

I couldn't sleep. Not after a day like today. Not after she had said my name like that. It was the first time she had called me Jackson and my name had never sounded so good. If we hadn't been in public I would have kissed her right then and there.

Can we mark her yet? Blaize whined.

"I don't know... there's still so much I don't know."

This is stupid and you know it. She's no danger to our pack. We NEED our mate! We can't be a proper Alpha without our Luna. She is everything we've ever wanted...

I knew he was right. I wanted her bad. I was beginning to need her like I needed air. Somehow in the span of three weeks I had become completely attached. But there was this nagging thought in the back of my mind that something wasn't right. That something from her past was going to put the pack in jeopardy. I fought the feeling, especially after getting to know her. There wasn't a mean bone in that woman's body.

"We'll just have to wait and see Blaize. Besides, I don't know if she's even ready for me to mark her- no matter how much we want to."

I thought back to the moment we had shared in the office. The way she felt pressed up against me, how she seemed to somehow fit perfectly in my arms. I could still feel her soft lips on mine.

I decided I'd talk to Jim tomorrow to see if he'd come up with anything else.

I woke in the morning with a bit of a spring in my step. When I made it in to work, as always, she was already there. "Good morning, Miss Lovett."

She smiled warmly at me, "Good morning, Mr. Thorpe." I was suddenly taken back to the day before and all I wanted was for her to say my name again.

She followed me in with a piece of paper, "You had a few early calls come in this morning. I told them you would call them when you came into the office. Mr. Talbot said he is looking for some private security for a banquet next week. I told him it was short notice for such a large event but he still wanted to speak with you."

"That's fine. I'll make these calls and then I have meeting at ten thirty."

"Yes, with Rose Enterprises. I'll let you know when they are here."

"Thank you, Miss Lovett." I looked up at her and the bright smile on her face. She gave a small nod before walking out of the room which I thoroughly enjoyed watching.

After my morning of phone calls and meetings I walked out of the office to see Sasha standing from her desk, checking her watch.

"Off to lunch?"

"Yep, hot date," she winked.

It was decided. I didn't like that. I could feel my eyes darken at the thought of her being out with some other man. Whoever this Paul guy was, I was on the verge of punching his face in. The elevator dinged and she swayed over. I watched as an old man stepped off, embracing her in a hug.

THAT'S Paul?! Blaize just about lost his mind. The guy had to be sixty, at least.

I suddenly realized I needed to fix my face when she turned back toward me and her expression dropped. She whispered to him and they walked back toward me.

"Mr. Thorpe, this is Paul Mariano. Paulie, this is Jackson Thorpe." I could see Sasha beaming as she introduced us, which only angered me more.

Paul held out a hand, giving me a firm handshake. "Mr. Thorpe, it's a pleasure to finally meet you. I don't think you understand how glad I was to have been hired on here, since I only have a few years left until retirement."

I heard a laugh and turned my face to see Sasha scoff at him, "Retire? You're not a day over thirty." She gave him a wink and he patted her hand.

He turned back to me with a smirk on his face, "Is she as much trouble to you as I think she is?"

"And then some," I laughed.

She scowled at both of us before leading him away, "I see how it is. You are supposed to be on my side, you old hound."

She turned back to me with a smile before leading him into the break room. After lunch I sat in my office, still steaming at the fact that she was lunching with a man three times her age.

Miss Lovett, my office.

A few minutes later there was a tap on the door. "Mr. Thorpe?"

"Come in," I said calmly.

I watched her walk in with a smile and stroll up to my desk. "What can I do for you?"

"Seriously?"

She looked at me with real confusion and I was irritated she couldn't see the problem here. "Seriously, what?"

"Paul?"

She smiled, "Isn't he the best? Well, apart from the moment you two ganged up on me."

"Sasha, he's triple your age!" I hollered. I winced, I didn't mean for it to sound so harsh.

She looked at me with a scowl. "And?"

I exhaled, trying to keep my cool, "And I thought I told you I didn't want you dating anyone else."

I watched Sasha as her eyes widened. She gasped before bursting out into laughter. Now I was confused. "Sasha, this isn't funny.. he-"

"Wait, did you think I'm ACTUALLY dating him?!"

I stopped speaking, trying to figure out where I had gone wrong.

"Jackson, I was teasing you!" She shook her head, "Gross! He's sixty! He's like a father to me!"

Embarrassed. That didn't even begin to describe how I felt. I could feel my cheeks flush. I closed my eyes and squished my face, "I think I misunderstood..." I opened my eyes when she quieted to see Sasha staring at me, her expression almost sad.

"Jackson, I found my mate. Why would I go dating someone?" she whispered. "I know you don't feel the pull as strongly as I do, but I believe in mates. I wouldn't go off with some other man after finding the only one I'm meant to be with."

My head snapped up at her words.

Does she think we don't want her?! I could hear Blaize panicking.

I stood from my desk and made my way over to Sasha. I cupped her face in my hands and brushed my lips against hers, kissing her slow and gentle. I didn't rush into her this time. I wanted her to know just how much I wanted her as my mate.

SEVENTEEN

JACKSON
I made my way down the hallway to Jim's office.
"Jimmy, you got a moment?" I asked as I poked my head through the door.

He swung around in his chair, "Always."

I sat down in the chair across from his desk and let out a deep breath. "Have you found anything else?"

He shook his head, "No. I've been looking everywhere. I can't seem to find where she came from or what had happened."

I sat back in the chair, ready to tell Jim everything I had found out. "I know what happened to her. Jim, it's real bad."

He leaned forward. "Do you know what pack it was?"

I shook my head, "No, she doesn't remember."

I repeated her story to him, telling him all about why they were exiled and what had happened to her mother. I told him about bouncing around with her father before finally settling. Being orphaned at sixteen and almost killed. Everything I had learned.

Jim sat back in his chair and ran his hand through his hair, "Man.. she was only four. She's been a rogue her entire life. I'm glad we found her."

I nodded, "But it also explains why she didn't go beast like other rogues. Her family were good people. She didn't choose this."

"I can't believe she survived all that." He looked up at me with a smirk, "She's going to make a strong Luna."

I rolled my eyes at him, "Is mating the only thing you think about?"

"Of course! Have you seen my mate? She's dynamite!" Jim roared, laughing loud when I looked at him in disgust. Jim rubbed his chin before leaning back in his chair, "I guess I can try and find a trail leading backwards from their time in Florida. See if I can find something."

"That maybe could work," I replied.

Jim nodded and we sat in silence for a few moments while he processed. Suddenly his head snapped up. His eyes were wide and I could see his face begin to pale.

"Jimmy, what's wrong?"

"Jack... what if... what if she's from our pack?"

I scoffed at him, "Jim, that's impossible. We would have known if she was from our pack."

"We don't know. We didn't check our own records. We just assumed she wasn't from here," Jim replied.

"No. The story she told me, the Alpha was a monster." I shook my head, not wanting to even think it.

"You and I both know Dad was awful. I don't even know how much mom shielded us from. He could have done it."

I squinted my eyes at him and shook my head, "No, because that would mean..."

Jim looked at me with sadness, "That would mean that Dad broke pack law, exiled her family, and had her mother killed."

EIGHTEEN

JACKSON

I rushed out of Jim's office to the elevator. I kept my head forward, knowing if I made eye contact with Sasha I wouldn't be able to hide my fear.

"She can't be from our pack," I whispered as I made my way out of the building.

I drove home to the pack house. If anyone would know, Mom would.

I bounded from my car and into the house, immediately mind-linking my mom, calling her to my office.

"Jackson, what's wrong?" she asked as she walked into the office. I knew she could sense my fear and anger.

"Mom, have a seat," I spoke quietly.

"Sweetheart, what is going on? Is everything okay? Is Jimmy?"

"Jim is fine, Mom," I replied.

She sighed in relief. I could feel her eyes on me but I knew I needed to collect myself before speaking to her. I moved around the desk and sat beside her. "Mom, I have some hard questions for you and I need you to tell me the truth."

She took my hand in hers and I could feel her warmth calm me. I was glad, I knew I would need a level head for this. "What's going on, Jackson?"

"Mom, do you remember the Lovett family? They would have lived here about twenty years ago."

"Lovett? As in..."

"Sasha, yes," I replied. I could see the confusion in her face.

"I don't remember there ever being a Lovett family in the pack, dear. But if they were rogues they might have changed their last name."

I nodded, realizing she was probably right. "Her parent's names were Elsie and Lucas."

She sat quietly for a moment, racking her brain for any scrap of remembrance. I watched as her eyes widened before looking up at me and letting out a gasp. "Reynolds. Their last name was Reynolds."

I froze. That wasn't the answer I wanted. I had been praying that she wouldn't know who they were, that there was no way Sasha had come from our pack. I could feel the heat rising within me. I walked into my file room and looked up their file. I sat down with it but was unable to open it. My mom took it from my hands and opened it.

"The Reynolds," she began, "Lucas, 23; Elsie, 23; Sasha, 4. Status: Exiled. Reason: Broke pack law. Refusal to obey and submit to orders directly from Alpha." I watched my mother shake her head, "That's not what happened."

I shook my head, "No. It's not." I could feel the anger pulsing through me. This had happened here. My pack. My father. The place I was proud to call home. The place I told her she was safe.

I stood up and bolted out of the room, ignoring the calls of my mother. I ran straight to the woods, not even bothering to strip before shifting. I sprinted hard, running as fast as I could through the forest.

What are we going to tell our mate? She's going to reject us, she's going to leave us. How the hell did this happen?! Blaize was just as angry as I was, and neither of us knew the answers to his questions. I ran for hours, trying to figure out how we would fix this. When I finally ran all the anger out of myself I went back home.

I walked into the pack house to see my mom still sitting there. I sat down beside her, my head in my hands, "What am I going to do?" I felt her healing touch calm me. I looked up at her to see tears in her eyes.

"This is my fault."

I shook my head, "No mom, this is on Dad. He was the monster, not you. He..."

"I should have stopped him. He was just so cruel. Thankfully he never hurt you or Jimmy. I would have killed him," she said with anger.

I laughed, "I know you would have." I looked forward as I tried to think back on my father. "He was a hard, mean man. I remember training under him, how harsh he was. It took me years to gain back the pack's trust. This isn't on us mom, it's on him. HE did this. And once again I'm stuck cleaning up his mess."

"What are you going to tell Sasha?"

I shrugged, "The truth. I can't hide this from her. She would never forgive me if I kept it from her. Granted, she might never forgive me if I do tell her."

My mother smiled reassuringly, "Yes, but that girl loves you. I can tell."

"I don't know if that's going to be enough. Her entire life is our fault. How could she become the Luna of the pack that exiled her, that killed her mother, that left her to fend for herself?"

"Do you want me there?"

"No," I replied, " It'll be better if I do it alone."

My mom gave my hand a squeeze before leaving me with my thoughts.

How did this happen? Blaize grumbled.

"How am I going to tell her?" I whispered to myself as I let out a long exhale. How was I supposed to hurt woman who had invaded most of my waking thoughts since the moment I met her?

NINETEEN

SASHA

When Jackson left this morning it was a bit curious. But I just assumed he had pressing issues back at the pack. If he needed anything he would call.

The end of the day came and went and he never came back. I stayed a bit later just in case, finishing up some work while I waited. Five thirty and nothing.

I walked home, taking advantage of the warm evening. When I got back to my apartment I found Jackson sitting outside the door.

"Well good evening, Mr. Thorpe," I smiled.

He looked up at me with a faint smile and I could tell something was wrong.

"What's the matter?" I asked with a knotted brow.

He shook his head at me, "Nothing. Can I come up? I have a few things to talk to you about."

I looked at him sideways, a bit hesitant at the request, but let him up. As we walked in I slipped out of my shoes, walking in heels all day was a little bit like torture. "Have a seat, let me change out of my work clothes really quick." I changed quickly into some leggings and a loose tee before joining him on the couch.

"Can I get you something? Water?"

He shook his head again, keeping his gaze lowered.

I had never seen him like this before and it was a bit worrying. "Jackson," I placed my hand on his arm sending tingles through my fingers, "Something is clearly wrong. Tell me, maybe I can help."

He let out a small laugh, "How are you so kind all of the time?"

"Would you rather I be mean? I can if you want me to. I'm real good at name calling," I teased.

He looked up at me, an emotion in his eyes that seemed to be affection mixed with sadness. "Can I just hold you for a minute?"

I looked at him curiously, hesitating for a moment before agreeing. He wrapped his arms around me and we ended up tangled into one another. Being close to him relaxed me and I could hear Raya purr in my head. He bent his head down and gently brushed his lips against mine, offering a deep, gentle kiss. He exhaled and released me.

"Okay Sasha, I need to tell you something. Something awful."

I watched him fidget with a ring on his finger and I could tell he was afraid to speak. "Jackson, what's the matter? You're starting to scare me."

"After you started working at TITAN I had Jim look into you. I needed to know you weren't a threat. After getting to know you I wanted to know more, I wanted to figure out where you had come from. We couldn't find anything, until..."

My eyes widened. They had found my old pack. I wasn't sure I was ready for this, "Jackson, what are you saying?"

He shook his head and met my eyes, "Sasha, your family is from my pack."

I snapped my face forward, trying to wrap my brain around what had just been said. "What do you mean I'm from your pack?"

"We had looked everywhere. Jim got this crazy idea in his head that maybe we couldn't find you because you were from here. But suddenly it all started making sense. When my mom confirmed it this morning I..."

"Your father..." I whispered. My wolf was fighting to get free, I was struggling to keep control. "Your father did this?"

He nodded, "My dad was a mean, cruel, horrible Alpha. It took me years to gain back the trust of the pack, to build it back up from the ruin my father had left it in."

"You're sure?" I growled.

"I am." He looked down, pulling a file from his jacket and handing it to me. "Your name is Sasha Reynolds. The reason given for your exile was because your parents broke pack law, disobeyed direct orders, and refused to submit- but we know that's not what happened."

I looked at the file, a picture of my family attached to the front page. I didn't have any pictures of my parents. They had all been lost when we were exiled. I could feel the anger building inside me as I ran my fingers across their faces. "I need you to leave."

"Sasha... I'm so sorry. I promised my pack was safe for you. I had no idea..."

"Leave," I spoke sternly, hoping he would get the hint. I needed to be alone. I needed to work through this.

"Sasha please..." he replied quietly. I looked up at him. His eyes were full of sadness and regret.

"Jackson, get out. I need... I need some time. I need to process this." I could feel the fire inside me. If he stayed I would say things I didn't mean. I needed time to wrap my head around it all.

He lowered his head before standing and walking to the door. "I'm sorry Sasha. Don't... don't push me away," he whispered as he left.

When the door closed I couldn't hold it anymore. The dam burst. I cried, my body heaving with sobs. How was I supposed to get past this? How could I look at my mate and not see his father killing my mother? How could I be his mate and live in his pack, the pack I was exiled from?

I woke the next morning, my tears had all been cried out and my cheeks were stiff. I got dressed and went to work. I knew I would have to see Jackson but I would do everything in my power to avoid being alone with him. I couldn't do this yet.

I heard the ding of the elevator and the pause in his step as he saw me. "Miss Lovett... you're here?" I could hear the worry and excitement in his voice.

"Yes, good morning Mr. Thorpe."

He walked into his office and I knew he was expecting me to follow but I wasn't going to.

Mr. Thorpe,

You have a conference call with Dunbar at nine thirty and then a lunch meeting in the conference room at twelve.

S. Lovett

I began on my work when I heard the familiar ding.

Thank you Sasha. I'm glad you came in today.

I closed my eyes and took a deep breath. "No Sasha. You can't go there. We need time."

Thankfully the day went by slowly. After lunch I came back to see him at my desk. "Can I help you, Mr. Thorpe?"

"My office please, Miss Lovett."

I attempted to calm myself. My plan to avoid him today had failed. I walked into his office and spoke quickly, "What can I do for you?"

"Sasha," he spoke quietly and stepped toward me. I stepped backward, not wanting to be any closer. He saw my actions and stopped, a scowl spreading on his face. "Sasha, I'm not going to hurt you."

"I know that." I looked at him, "But I need some time."

"What do you mean by time?" he asked. I could hear the anger creeping into his voice.

"Exactly that. I need time. I need to get my head straight, to wrap my head around all of this. I just found out my mate and future pack is actually my old pack and my mate's father is the reason for everything that has happened in my life. Jackson, I just need time."

He let out a slow breath, "If that's what you want."

"Yes, it is," I said sternly. I turned and left the room, trying not to let him see the tears that were threatening to fall.

TWENTY

JACKSON

Sasha closed the door behind her and I began to lose control. I could feel Blaize fighting to get out, he was angry and he wanted his mate. We both did. I no longer cared about her past, I just wanted her. And now it might be too late.

I turned to the desk and gripped the sides, fighting the overwhelming urge to shift. "I need to get out of here," I mumbled, knowing if I lost it here at work there would be hell to pay. I mind-linked Jim, "Jimmy, I'm heading to basement containment."

"Containment?! Jack, are you okay? Wait for me and I'll walk you down, make sure you get there before shifting."

Suddenly Jim was bursting into my office and grabbing me by the shirt. I caught Sasha's gaze as he ran me to the elevator. I could see the hurt and worry in her eyes. It wasn't helping.

Jim entered the code for the basement and we stood in silence as I tried to rein it in. The ride down to the basement felt like years. When the doors finally dinged I felt Jim grab me again and push me down the corridor. A moment later he fumbled with the keypad before opening the door and pushing me into one of the rooms. We had built these for occasions like this. We couldn't risk having a building full of wolves in the middle of the city and not have a plan for a situation like this. We didn't have to use them very often, usually just when some of the security teams lost their cool.

The cells were solid concrete and the only way in or out was the cell door. On the inside it was coated in silver so that we couldn't wolf out and then break out.

I stood in the center of the room attempting to calm my breathing when I felt Blaize making it through. I shifted and he jumped forward before howling and pacing the room. We were both upset over the possibility of losing Sasha but he was more than that, Blaize was angry. I could feel the fire inside him. After almost thirty minutes of pacing I could feel him begin to calm down.

"Blaize, buddy we can't hulk out every time she gets us riled up. You know she has to process this, no matter how much we hate it."

We are going to lose her and it's your fault. We should have marked her the first day we met her! He yelled at me, his frustration still raw.

"You know we couldn't do that..."

I could feel him calm down and finally hand back control. I shifted back and yelled for Jim when I knew I was good. He opened the door and threw some clothes at me before leaning against the concrete wall. "So are you going to tell me what the hell that was?"

"Nothing," I replied bluntly.

Jim pushed off the wall and stepped toward me, "THAT was not nothing. You never lose control like that, Jackson! You almost shifted in the middle of the office! You're the Alpha, you can't pull that crap! So what happened man?"

"Sasha..." I lowered my face, I didn't want to let him see how upset this had all made me.

"Sasha, what?"

I growled, I didn't want to talk about this, "Just.. Sasha! It's not your business."

"You made it my business. Now do I need to go talk to Sasha or are you going to tell me?"

"She called things off." I let out a long breath hoping it would steady me, "She told me she needs time, that she doesn't want to be with me until she gets all of this straight."

"Did she reject you?" Jim met my eyes and I could see he was worried.

I shook my head, "No, but I can't be sure that isn't where it's headed."

Jim placed a hand on my shoulder, "I'm sorry, brother. I don't think she'll do it though, I can see how much she's warmed up to you just in the last few weeks."

I shrugged, "I don't think she knows just how much I want her. I fought the pull so hard and now that I've opened myself up to her I'm going to lose her."

Jim laughed, "Well then show her! You can't just sulk around until she decides she wants you. Show her just how different you are from Dad."

"I guess," I shrugged. We made our way back upstairs and when we exited the elevator I could see she was staring, trying to figure out what had happened. She was worried.

"Worried is good right?" I smirked internally. My comment was met by a pouty huff from Blaize and I stepped forward.

"Miss Lovett," I said as I walked past her desk.

"Mr. Thorpe." She didn't even look at me. But as I looked down at Sasha, her long blonde hair falling to her face and framing her bright hazel eyes, I got lost. I could smell her, that honeysuckle and vanilla was intoxicating and I wanted to breathe her in. I had been fighting it for so long, now all I wanted was to make up for lost time and take her right here and now.

I don't know how long I'll be able to do this, especially when she smells so good and looks like that. I quickly walked into my office and collapsed at my desk. There was no way I was getting anything done today. My self-pitying was interrupted when the phone rang. "Yes?"

"Mr. Thorpe, you have Ted Smith on line one." Sasha's voice was emotionless and I didn't like how it sounded. I didn't like this cold front.

"Thank you," was all I managed to reply. I knew she didn't want to talk to me. She sat on the line for a moment, as though she wanted to say something more before hanging up and leaving me alone again.

At the end of the day I gathered my things and walked out of my office. "Goodnight, Miss Lovett."

"Goodnight," she replied stiffly.

I was running circles in my head, trying to find some excuse to be near her but I couldn't think of anything.

We need a plan to get her back..

"Tomorrow..." I replied, "Tomorrow we will start work on getting back our mate."

TWENTY ONE

SASHA

Jim practically sprinted down the hall, past me, and into Jackson's office. Suddenly they were both dashing back down the hall to the elevator. I saw Jackson's face, his eyes darkening. He couldn't control his wolf, he was about to shift right there in the office.

"Did we do that?"

We couldn't have.. Raya replied distantly as though she was trying to figure it out herself.

"Right.." I replied quietly, not sure if I believed myself. I couldn't help but wonder and be worried.

An hour later he came back up, the same composed Alpha he always was. Maybe I had read it all wrong.

You shouldn't be caring hun. You know what his pack did to us, to our family. We should just leave this place...

I knew Raya wasn't serious. She was just upset about this whole situation. She wanted him even more than I did, she wanted a pack and a home. I knew I would have to take some time to figure out if I could get past this and forgive his people and his family.

Thankfully, tomorrow Jackson wouldn't be here and I wouldn't have to be near him all day. "Maybe I should just quit.." I thought before shaking my head. I needed this job. There was no way I could leave unless I found something to replace it. Maybe I should put out some feelers.

Thursday went by quickly. I thought I had escaped having to deal with all of this until I was ambushed at the end of the day.

"Sasha!" Jim hollered as the elevator doors began to close. I held them open and he jogged inside. "Thanks. On your way home?"

I nodded with a smile. I didn't want to have the conversation I knew was coming.

"So how are you doing?"

There it was. I exhaled, "I'm okay."

"Are you really? Sasha, I want you to know that we had no idea. We knew our dad was a cruel man, but we had no idea something like what happened to you had ever occurred in our pack. If Jackson had been Alpha..."

"If Jackson had been Alpha none of that would have happened," I cut in.

Jim smiled down at me, "My big brother is stubborn and sometimes a grump, but he isn't cruel."

"I know."

Jim looked at the floor and kicked at some imaginary dust, "He told me about what happened. I'm sorry you don't feel safe in our pack or with us."

I snapped my head up, "It's not that. It's just..."

"It's a lot to digest. I get it," he added.

I liked Jim, I didn't want to hurt his feelings. The truth was I didn't know how I felt about any of this and I couldn't further complicate it with adding my feelings for Jackson. I gave him a smile and a "goodnight" before heading home.

Friday morning came and I groaned at the thought of having to go in to work. "Can we just call in?" I whined as I stood in the shower, letting the hot water rinse off all of my exhaustion.

If we don't show up, he might come looking for us. Do you really want him here?

My eyes widened. Being alone with him in my apartment was the last thing I wanted. "Work it is then."

Just as I sat on my desk the elevator dinged. Jackson made his way toward me, his gray suit fitting him perfectly and emphasizing every part of his muscular frame.

"Good morning, Miss Lovett."

"Good morning, Mr. Thorpe." I didn't follow him in today. I couldn't be alone with him.

Mr. Thorpe,

**Your 9am should be here any minute. Would you
like to meet with them in your office or in the
conference room?**

S. Lovett

I watched my computer waiting for a reply.

**In here is fine. Can you bring in a pot of coffee
please?**

I let out a sigh and made my way to the kitchen before filling
a thermal pot with coffee and placing it on a tray along with
several cups. I walked into his office and caught his eye so I
gave him a small smile. He was sitting at his desk going
through some files, so I placed the tray on the coffee table
before making my way back out. I went to open the door
when suddenly it was pushed shut. I could feel him behind
me, his body close to mine as he leaned against his hands
placed on the door. It made my breath catch.

"I know you don't want to over-complicate things for
yourself right now and I understand that," Jackson's voice
was almost a whisper, husky and low. "Just know this Sasha,
I'm sorry for this and I miss you." His breathy words left
warmth on my cheek and suddenly the warmth was gone as

he stepped away from me. I quickly left his office and just about collapsed at my desk. Once his meeting came in I decided I needed some air. I walked out of the building and sat on a bench outside.

"Well hey there, hun."

I looked up and smiled at my favorite person. "Hey, Paulie."

"You look like you've got a lot on your mind." He sat down next to me with worry in his eyes.

I shrugged, "I just found some new information about where my family came from. Things are complicated. My past is complicated."

"Well, then make it less complicated."

I let out a scoff, "It's not that easy."

"But your past can't be changed. Take what you've learned and grow from it. Don't let it ruin what you have going for you."

I chuckled, "I don't have much going for me, Paul."

He let out a surprised laugh, "You have plenty my girl! You have a great job, a great home, and I'm pretty sure our boss is sweet on you." He winked at me with a nudge and I laughed.

I ran my hand through my hair, "Thanks, Paul. Alright, I should head back up, I don't want to miss anything important."

He patted my knee and walked back in with me. As I sat back down Jackson's meeting ended and he motioned for me to come in.

"Can I get you something, Mr. Thorpe?"

"Yes, theres a group of files under the name Macy. Can you grab them for me?"

"Yes. Anything else?"

Jackson turned to me and smiled, "Yes. You look beautiful today."

I know for a fact that my face held everything from desire and appreciation to fear and confusion. I didn't know how to respond. He had never been so attentive. "I.. uhh.. Thank you." I turned to leave and I am almost certain I heard a low growl escape his lips before I closed the door.

"What the hell was that?" I muttered, hoping nobody would walk by and see me so flustered.

Mate wants us... Raya whispered. I was surprised, she had been so angry and hurt like I was. But she was a wolf and she wanted her mate. Now I just had to figure out if I wanted him too.

TWENTY TWO

JACKSON

Three weeks had gone by. I had done everything short of kissing that girl. I had flirted shamelessly and made random kind remarks toward her. I was not about to let her forget that I wanted her, that she was my mate and I would do everything to make sure she knew I cared and that she was safe with me.

It was Thursday and even though I wasn't at the office, I knew she was.

Good morning Sasha,

I have need of you this afternoon. Just some administrative work at the pack house.

Thanks, Jackson

I hadn't even thought it through. I knew I'd need a reason to have her come in. I began to be worried when almost ten minutes went by with no response. I sighed in relief when she finally messaged back.

I don't think that's a good idea.

That was slightly irritating. Apparently I couldn't play nice cop on this one.

Miss Lovett,

I might remind you that this is part of your job as my assistant. I need you to be here by 1:30.

Thank you, Jackson Thorpe.

I sat back in my chair, irritated that I had to play the boss card just to get her here. I knew why she was hesitating, but I also knew she would have to face this at some point.

Let's just hope she doesn't choose to quit on you instead of coming down...

"Thank you. That's really helpful, Blaize," I replied sarcastically. "Now I just need to find a reason for why I called her here."

I shuffled around the office, mixing up files and trying to figure out if there were any pack meetings coming up.

A few hours later I looked at my watch. Two o'clock. I scowled, she didn't come. I stepped out of my office and heard a familiar sound. I followed it and entered the pack kitchen where her scent hit me. I looked around the room and my eye caught her sitting at a table with my mother and Ashley. I laughed to myself knowing she was probably here on time before being ambushed by those two.

I walked over to them with a smirk, "Shirking our duties I see."

Sasha glanced up, her eyes were less bright than normal. I knew she had mixed feelings about being here.

"Nonsense!" my mother chimed. "We were talking shop."

I saw Ashley give Sasha a wink, which obviously meant they were talking about literally everything else. It made me smile that they had opened themselves to her. They had been smart. I shouldn't have been so stubborn, so closed off.

"Well Miss Lovett, ready to do some work?" I asked and she stood from the bench which received complaints from the two other women.

"Fine," my mother sulked, "But you're staying for dinner."

I could see Sasha try to protest but I knew how good my mother was, she wasn't about to take no for an answer.

As we made our way back into the office I gave her a smile, "Thank you for coming back. I know you don't want to be here."

She shrugged, "You didn't give me much of a choice."

I flinched at that one. It reminded me of how my father had just expected others to do his will and the thought that I had done that bothered me a little. I chose to ignore it though. I knew whatever my reaction was would just distance her more. I ran my hand through my hair and sat down, "So there's a bunch of files that need to be gone through and I have a couple of events coming up with reminders that need to go out."

"I'll do the files first, then we can sit down and talk about event details, if that's alright," she replied as she looked at the little mess of folders I had made.

"Sounds good. I have to go meet some pack contractors about some new houses so I'll be back in about an hour." I stood to go, hesitating at the door before turning back to her. "Sasha, I know you want to hate me, but I'm not going to give up on you."

She snapped her head up to me, her eyes meeting mine. She softened for a moment, revealing her struggle. I didn't need or want a response, so I left to let her stew on my words.

"How is it going in there?" A familiar voice spoke from behind me as I exited the pack house. I turned to my mother who was sitting on a chair on the front porch.

I shrugged, "It's going."

"That girl has so much struggle going on," she frowned and I knew my mom had felt her. "But oddly enough most of her struggle isn't about the past, but how to proceed with the future."

"So she doesn't know if she wants me." I shook my head, frustrated at the situation.

My mother shrugged before standing and cupping my face in her hands, "If I had known who your father would have become I would have rejected him when we met. I couldn't protect our pack and I regret that every day. But you are NOT him and she sees that. She just has to figure out if she can make a life here."

I gave her a small smile before heading out to the new houses. She had given me a bit of hope.

"Okay, so for the pack meeting you just need an email reminder sent out. Are you doing anything after that needs planning?"

"No, just the meeting this time. But we do need to start plans on the start of summer party. It's just a few months away and it's a big deal here."

As we planned, Sasha wrote all her notes down, offering advice when needed. Even if she didn't end up as my mate I hoped she would still stay as my PA, she was the best one I'd had in a long time.

"Well it's just about time for dinner, should we call it a day?"

She nodded, "I should really go though."

I laughed, "Oh no you don't. If you leave I'll have to deal with the wrath of my mother AND Ashley."

Sasha giggled and it made my heart jump at the sound. It was the first little bit of warmth I'd seen in weeks. She had kept herself so distant, so shut down, that I thought all of this might have broken her. I knew better, she had survived so much.

We sat down in the dining hall next to Mom, Ashley, Jim, and their new little pup. My mom was completely obsessed and was more than happy to hold her throughout dinner. I enjoyed sitting next to Sasha, feeling the warmth of her body near mine. Once in a while our arms would brush against each other sending shocks up my arm. It was taking all of me to not grab her and kiss the hell out of her. I tempted fate a little halfway through dinner and took her hand for a moment, squeezing it so she would know I wanted to be near her even if it was just for a moment. I regretted it immediately because when I released her hand I craved the touch again. Blaize wasn't very happy about it either. He whined for ten minutes afterward, telling me to take her hand back. But I wasn't going to push my luck.

Then dinner ended and she left, leaving me feel empty as I watched her drive away.

TWENTY THREE

SASHA

When I arrived at the pack house I hesitated again, but this time it wasn't out of fear. I knew spending the day with him would be hard.

"Sasha! You're here! Jackson didn't say you were coming out today." I turned around to see Amalia walking up to the house. She embraced me with a warm, soothing hug as her healing powers radiated off of her. "But I'm glad you did. Come inside and see my new grandpup!"

I smiled, Jim had told me that Ashley had given birth to their little girl. He had shown me pictures and she was adorable.

Amalia and I walked in together and we sat down next to Ashley in the dining hall. "Sasha!" Ashley smiled to me and gave me a hug as well. I had to admit, even with my reservations, I felt welcome here. "I'm so glad you're here."

"Ashley, you look amazing for just having had a baby." I smiled before my eyes rested on the bundle in her arms, "And this must be Penny! She is even cuter in person." I couldn't help but squish my face at her, I loved babies. We chatted for a bit about life and the happenings in the pack and such. Then Amalia turned to me with a saddened look, "Sasha..."

I knew where this was headed. Amalia had been around when I had been exiled, she had been mated to that man. I didn't know if I'd be able to get through talking about this with her. I met her eyes and I could see all of the sadness and regret.

"Sasha, I'm so sorry." She looked down at the floor and I could see the tears welling in her eyes. "Jackson's father was a cruel man. If I had known what he did... when I found out it was days later. I was so angry. But he was stronger than me and I had my boys to look out for. I'm so sorry for everything that happened because I was too weak to challenge him."

I felt horrible. I didn't even think about the cruelty she must have faced as his mate or the fear she must have had knowing he was hurting their pack and there was nothing she could do. I hugged her tightly, "Amalia, it wasn't your fault. I won't lie and say I didn't blame you a little. But I know how kind and soft you are, you wouldn't have knowingly let my family be harmed like that."

I released her and searched her face, offering a reassuring smile. She let out a sad chuckle as she wiped her tears, "How is it that you were the one hurt and yet I'm crying?"

I smiled and gave her a wink, "I did all my crying at home."

"So what are you going to do about Jackson?"

My head flipped around to Ashley. Her face was stiff as she waited for my reply.

"Honestly, I don't know. I know it wasn't his fault, I mean he couldn't have been more than six years old. I can't blame him for what happened to my family. But.."

Ashley nodded, "I understand. You can't be sure."

Amalia took my hand, "But when can you ever be sure when it comes to opening yourself up to another person?"

I shrugged, "I guess I can't. But I mean, there's so much that has happened to me because of this pack. How can I trust them?"

Ashley shrugged, "You can trust them. The pack that exiled your family isn't the pack you see today. And that's all because of Jackson. He has worked so hard to make this pack a safc placc." Shc pauscd and I could scc shc was hesitating, trying to decide if she wanted to continue. "It seems to me that you need to figure out what you know and what you want. And then act on it."

I nodded, "I know I do."

We all smiled warmly at each other, glad we had talked it out and came out the other side as friends. I didn't realize how long we had been talking until Jackson found us. I knew he was there before he spoke, I could smell that intense scent of his and it clouded my mind.

Spending the rest of the day with him was just as hard as I thought it would be. Every fiber of my wolf wanted to just jump on him and kiss him to death. But I knew I had some work to do on myself first. And when he walked me out to my car I wanted so badly for him to hold me. But he respected my wishes like he always did. I appreciated that, knowing if he had pulled me in to him I wouldn't have been able to stop it.

TWENTY FOUR

SASHA

All weekend all I did was slump on the couch. In my comfy pajamas and cheesy movies, I wallowed for two days. I had gone from having mostly accepted how my life had turned out to having to confront everything all over again.

These things I knew for certain:

My family were once members of Jackson's pack.

His father, an abusive and cruel Alpha, exiled my family unlawfully because he didn't like that my father challenged him.

Instead of just exiling us, he sent protectors after us and killed my mother.

My father and I barely made ends meet for the rest of our lives, alone and worried humans would catch us shifting.

I was left alone at sixteen when my father died.

I dug myself out of my hole and made a place for myself. I didn't need a pack, I was all the pack I would ever need.

And yet when I thought about it...

I wanted to be able to shift and run whenever I wanted.

I wanted to hate the entire pack, but I couldn't. I knew I couldn't hold what that horrible man had done against them.

I wanted to belong to something.

And I wanted Jackson.

I growled to myself, "What am I going to do?"

IS THIS EVEN A QUESTION? I THINK WE'VE PUNISHED HIM AND OURSELVES LONG ENOUGH, AND I THINK WE'VE GONE LONG ENOUGH WITHOUT A HOME. Raya seemed to know I wanted to go back to him. But could I trust them?

TWENTY FIVE

SASHA

"Good day, Mr. Thorpe," I said happily. Following some serious time sulking and profound thought I had come out from my dim spot and concluded I expected to push ahead.

Jackson halted before my work area, presumably in shock from the reality I had addressed him first. "Hello, Miss Lovett," he stammered.

I followed him in to his office and put a few grinds down around his work area. "These all need last endorsement before I send them down to arranging. What's more your ten o'clock meeting has been pushed back to eleven. Do you need me to arrange some lunch for it?"

He gazed at me with his eyes wide. I felt awful tossing back in like this all of a sudden. In any case, I needed to concede, I appreciated watching him wriggle.

"Mr Thorpe?" I asked, a little smile advancing onto my face.

"I.. ummm.. indeed. Lunch would be fine."

I gestured and left the room, leaving him in a puddle of disarray.

"Hello, Sasha," Jim sang as he moved toward my work area.

"Good day, Beta Jim," I grinned.

He fixed as disarray spread across his face. "You're terribly cheerful earlier today."

I shook my head, "No, I'm almost certain this is simply me."

Jim shook his head prior to going to the workplace, "Is Jackson ready?"

"Indeed, he just arrived."

He gestured his head and gave me an odd look prior to entering Jackson's office. I was appreciative for the flimsy dividers as I got a fantastic view to their little conversation.

"What's new with Sasha?"

"I can't really understand. I came in today and she was very much like that." I laughed at Jackson's disarray.

"Does this mean she is over it? That she doesn't despise you?"

"I have no clue brother..."

At the point when they began discussing work I quit tuning in, picking to focus all alone. I tapped on the entryway in the wake of getting the call that his customers were here. "Mr Thorpe?"

"Miss Lovett, come in." He waved at me as he got done with composing something into a record. He met my eyes cheerfully, "Okay, what do you want?"

"I was simply illuminating you that your customers are on their way up."

He stood up and attached the buttons on his suit coat, "Great." He followed me out of his office similarly as the lift ringed and the entryways opened. He drove them into the gathering room and they started their gathering. At eleven 45 the lunch request showed up and I took it in on a truck and set up the food on the back table as they proceeded with their gathering. I gave Jackson a gesture illuminating him it was prepared. "OK honorable man, everything smells too lovely, how about we snatch some food and continue will we?"

I strolled toward the entryway when I was halted, "Miss Lovett, would you be able to remain and take notes?"

I gave him a gesture, "Indeed, let me get my things." When I went into the room again I sat in the corner and started my work taking notes on the rest of the gathering. I was passing on in there. I wasn't ready to take my mid-day break and the gathering had eaten the entirety of the food. I was starving. I felt my stomach thunder at me and I admired see Jackson taking a gander at me sideways. I gave him a tight grin prior to returning to my work, trusting the gathering would end soon. At last, as we strolled them back to the lift I let out a moan prior to strolling back to my work area.

I was alarmed when a crate was put before me. "Eat." I admired see Jackson squinting his eyes at me.

"I'm fine, Mr. Thorpe."

Jackson let out a giggle, "I could hear your stomach from across the room."

I feigned exacerbation, "Fine."

He stood straight, glad for his little triumph, and strolled once more into his office. I liked the way that he actually needed to deal with me.

By the day's end I strolled in to his office, "Mr Thorpe?"

He turned upward from his work area and in the wake of seeing me with each of my things peered down at his watch, "Gracious gosh, I didn't understand what time it was."

I watched him bobble with his papers briefly as I attempted to assemble my boldness. I took a full breath and ventured forward, "Jackson."

He gobbled his head up and met my eyes with his.

"Please accept my apologies. I realize I shouldn't have
faulted you or your pack for what occurred. I shouldn't have
driven you away and rebuffed you for what your father did.
I just... Please accept my apologies."

I stopped briefly, checking his response. He remained there
stuck to the spot. Abruptly he adjusted the work area and
limited toward me, shutting the distance between us.
Jackson stood close, our appearances just inches separated.
"Sasha. Try not to apologize, you don't have anything to be
upset for. I ought to have made you mine the moment I met
you. I was a simpleton. Pardon me."

I grinned up at him, looking into his gem blue eyes. I arrived
at my hand up to cup his cheek and I experienced the glow
of his skin transmit through my hand.

I inclined forward and brushed his lips with mine, the sensation sending shockwaves through my entire body. I kissed him more profound, touching off the energy I had felt for him for the months we had known one another. Jackson yielded, folding his arms over me and pulling me close. Our lips squashed into each other as we tangled ourselves into one another. He supported my face, kissing my lips down to my jaw and following down my neck. He got me, my legs folded over his midriff and he conveyed me to the lounge chair, unfastening my skirt as he held me. He laid me down and moved above me, his hands playing with the buttons on my pullover as I bobbled with his belt. In the wake of losing all our garments Jackson moved gradually, putting kisses along my neck and shoulder where my imprint ought to be. I let out a groan as he kissed and sucked. I ran my give over his chest, feeling each chorded muscle and the smooth, warm skin that set my fingers ablaze each time I contacted him. Jackson kissed his direction down my body. He halted at my bosom, bringing each into his mouth prior to kissing down my stomach. He let his tongue bother my external dividers, making me groan again prior to sucking my bud, the sensation driving me wild. He slid his fingers inside me, making me curve my back in delight as he took his fingers in and out, the strain developing. "Jackson, I want you inside me.." I stammered, I could feel myself on the edge. He let out a snarl prior to moving back up my body, endeavoring to kiss every last trace of me. "Jackson..." I groaned as he squashed his lips to mine, our tongues taking in the flavor of one another. Jackson prodded me with his tip, creeping me out.

"My mate," he murmured as he kissed where he was intended to check me.

Jackson pushed inside me gradually, and we both groaned as we felt one another. I delved my fingers into his back, needing more. He kissed me with enthusiasm as he moved above me, pushing himself in and out as we both felt our pleasure building. We were overpowered by extraordinary delight as we both delivered.

As we held each other on the lounge chair I could feel happiness wash through me. This was the place where I was intended to be. Jackson inclined down and kissed my lips tenderly. "Sasha, I guarantee I will guard you for the remainder of our lives. Return home with me."

I grinned, believing that from this point forward this man was my home.

TWENTY SIX

JACKSON

"Hello, Mrs. Thorpe."

"Goodmorning, Mr. Thorpe."

It had been fourteen days since we had made up and two days since the Luna function. I was in paradise. She was all that I had longed for and she was turning into an astonishing Luna. She had been reluctant from the beginning however squeezed herself into the pack and everybody totally cherished her. It wasn't difficult to do, she was astonishing.

She followed me in to the workplace, discussing the gatherings for the afternoon and the calls I expected to return. I watched her as I sat on the edge of my work area. She was staggering. From the highest point of her shirt I could see her imprint and it caused me to solidify simply pondering the amount I needed to suck that spot. Her little pencil skirt was embracing my beloved spots as a whole and I looked as she battled a wanderer piece of hair that continued to fall into her face. I grinned and pushed off the work area to stroll toward her. I tucked the hair behind her ear and kissed her cheek. "You are excellent today."

She gave me a saucy grin, "You generally say that when I wear this skirt. Assuming I didn't have the foggiest idea about any better I'd say you just needed me for my body." She gave me a wink and dismissed to walk.

I got her from behind and folded my arms over her abdomen. I inclined right up front and murmured in her ear, "And assuming I didn't have a clue about any better I'd think you realized I like that skirt and wore it deliberately."

Sasha giggled brilliantly prior to pushing me. "You dog. You better stop before my supervisor discovers. He's a genuine killjoy."

I snarled, "I bet he'll concur with me." I turned her around to confront me and pulled her nearby. "When's my first gathering?"

"Ten thirty."

"Great," I grinned, tapping the lock on my office entryway as I inclined down to put my lips on hers. She laughed into my kiss prior to inclining in to me. I unfastened her skirt from the back and allow it to slide down her legs to the floor prior to slipping her shirt over her head. She loosened the buttons on my shirt and pushed it over my shoulders, allowing it to fall too. I pushed everything around my work area to the side and got her, putting her down on the work area. She played with my jeans as I kissed her neck, and I was astounded when my lump sprang free as she opened my jeans. I realized she was prepared for me, I could smell her excitement. I kissed down her neck, inclining her back so I could accept in her entire body as I followed kowtowed and down her middle. I sucked on my imprint, making her groan in joy. She sat up and dropped her give over my body and started to stroke my length, making me shudder in rapture. I was unable to stand by any more extended, I basically ripped her undies off and drove myself into her. She let out an uproarious groan which just made me insane. I push into her over and over as we both felt the strain fabricate. She came, groaning my name as she did. I felt delight overwhelm me as I delivered. I kissed her imprint and afterward her lips.

Later our little tryst around my work area we got ourselves dressed and Sasha approached me. She inclined in and kissed me profoundly prior to pulling ceaselessly, "Return to work, Mr. Thorpe."

"Indeed, Luna," I answered as I kissed her cheek.

She gave me a grin before she left, the swing of her hips
previously making me mix once more.

"I love you, Sasha."

Sasha went to me and grinned, "I love you too, Jackson."
I hope you like it
Please review and comment it

THANK YOU

www.ingramcontent.com/pod-product-compliance
Lightning Source LLC
Chambersburg PA
CBHW061536120726
48001CB00004B/1585